'Jared? Would you like your pancake now? Or later?'

A faint twitch to his lips, he said softly, 'Will the mixture keep?'

A *double entendre*? Yes, of course it was! Lian's eyes sparkling with delight at finding someone willing to play, she gave a slow, slightly wicked smile. 'Oh, yes,' she agreed, her voice deliberately husky, 'and mixture is often better left to stand. Don't you think?'

Dear Reader

The background in which a novel is set can be very important to a reader's enjoyment of the story. What type of background do you most enjoy? Do you like a story set in a large international city or do you prefer your story to be set in a quiet rural village away from the hustle and bustle of everyday life? What about exotic locations with hot climates and steamy lifestyles? Let us know and we'll do all we can to get you the story you want!

The Editor

Emma Richmond was born during the War in north Kent when, she says, 'Farms were the norm and motorways non-existent. My childhood was one of warmth and adventure. Amiable and disorganised, I'm married with three daughters, all of whom have fled the nest— probably out of exasperation! The dog stayed, reluctantly. I'm an avid reader, a compulsive writer and a besotted new granny. I love life and my world of dreams, and all I need to make things complete is a housekeeper— like, yesterday!'

Recent titles by the same author:

A STRANGER'S TRUST
DELIBERATE PROVOCATION

FATE OF
HAPPINESS

BY

EMMA RICHMOND

MILLS & BOON LIMITED
ETON HOUSE   18-24 PARADISE ROAD
RICHMOND   SURREY   TW9 1SR

*First published in Great Britain 1992
by Mills & Boon Limited*

© *Emma Richmond 1992*

*Australian copyright 1992
Philippine copyright 1992
This edition 1992*

ISBN 0 263 77725 1

*Set in Times Roman 10½ on 12 pt.
01-9209-51223 C*

Made and printed in Great Britain

CHAPTER ONE

TALL and slender, her long brown hair knotted loosely on top of her head, Lian—as in 'Lion'—leaned thankfully against the solitary lamppost that marked the crossroads. It was very hot. Shifting her position slightly to ease the ache in her back, she gazed around her at the unending vista of countryside. Not a dwelling to be seen. So which way now, clever clogs? Left or right? Straight on, or go back? What she should have done, of course, was waited at the station, only waiting around was not something she was very good at—nor was finding Haddon Lane, she admitted with a wry smile.

'Hello.'

With a little start, she swung round, and her grey eyes widened in astonishment as she stared down at the young boy who had addressed her. 'Good lord, where did you spring from? You frightened me half to death.'

'Sorry,' he apologised.

He didn't look sorry, he looked utterly and enchantingly mischievous. He was also absolutely filthy, as though he'd been bathing in mud. With a grin that was as wide and enchanting as his own, she observed, 'Well, at least you look as though you've been enjoying yourself.'

'Yeah, and Dad is going to do his pieces!' he admitted cheerfully. 'He told me to stay clean.'

5

'I don't think you succeeded,' she pointed out with an irrepressible chuckle.

His grin wider, if that were possible, he looked down at himself, then gave a shrug. 'Where are you going?' he asked curiously.

'Now that, young man, is most definitely the question. I was supposed to be going for an interview, but because the train was late, and there was no one waiting to meet me at the station, I thought, in my wisdom, that it might be better to walk——'

'Station?' he interrupted with a look of excitement. 'Hey, are you the one we've been waiting for? Wow! Dad's improving by the minute! We were beginning to think you weren't coming!'

'Dad?' she queried.

'Yeah! He's been up and down to the station all morning. That's why I was supposed to stay clean! This is great,' he declared enthusiastically. 'Come on!' Grabbing her hand, he began urging her along the lane to the left.

'Hold on, hold on,' she cautioned, 'I can't walk that fast, and I'm not altogether sure we aren't at cross purposes. No mention was made of a boy...'

'No, well, it wouldn't, would it?' he demanded with an adult air that was comical to say the least. 'Otherwise you might not have come.'

Successfully diverted, Lian queried in amusement, 'Why wouldn't I have come?'

'Because I'm difficult, of course. No one ever stays,' he added with obvious pride.

'Hm. Like that, is it?' He certainly looked as though he might be a handful, but definitely appealing. Shaking her head at him, and automatically forcing his pace to match her slower one, she wondered if that was why the agency had been so sparing with details. Certainly no mention had been made of a father and son, only one lady of indeterminate age. 'I thought Mrs Popplewell lived on her own...'

'Mrs... Hey! Look at that!' he interrupted, dragging her to a halt.

Following the line of his pointing finger, Lian stared rather blankly at some bushes. 'What?'

'It's gone now,' he said dismissively as he tugged her into action once more. 'It was a fox.'

'Oh.'

'Why can't you walk very fast?' he enquired with the bluntness of childhood.

'Because I hurt my back,' she said, rather more shortly than she intended.

Halting once more, he stared up at her, a frown on his quite abominably dirty face. 'Does that mean you can't do things? Like climb trees and stuff?'

No mention of sympathy, or a query as to how she had hurt it, only the important question of how it might affect himself, she thought with a helplessly wry smile. 'Yes, it does.' But oh, how I wish... Determinedly burying those thoughts because they did no good, except make her feel bitter, she murmured, 'I don't even know your name.'

'Simon.' After wiping his palm down his jean leg, he proffered it.

Solemnly shaking his hand, she introduced herself. 'Lian.'

With another wide grin, he encouraged cheerfully, 'Not much further. You should have turned right just after the station,' he added informatively. 'You walked the long way round.'

'So it seemed,' she said drily.

With a little laugh, he continued happily, 'You're much nicer than the last one; she was awful, really gross!' Halting by a gate, he swung it wide. 'Come on.'

With a bewildered little shake of her head, Lian followed him up the rather overgrown path towards a square little cottage, and then round the back to the wide cobbled yard. A mud-spattered Land Rover was parked askew beside what looked like a stable block.

'Hello, can I help you?'

Turning, Lian stared at the young woman framed in the open back door.

'Oh, hello,' she smiled. 'Are you Mrs Popplewell?'

'Mrs who?' she asked on a startled laugh.

'Popplewell.'

'Good heavens, no! I live next door, but what a precious name. Conjures up a rosy-cheeked old lady with soft grey hair, doesn't it? Apples and countryside, a cottage garden?'

'Yes,' Lian agreed with a rather bewildered smile, and if this woman lived next door, as she so obviously did, she must surely have known Mrs P, so why the startled laugh? 'Don't you...?'

'And she's probably fat and fifty with dyed hair and a harsh voice,' the woman laughed, clearly not in the least curious as to who Mrs Popplewell might be, or why Lian would be enquiring after her. Moving her eyes past the confused Lian, she gave an exclamation of horror. 'Simon! What on earth have you been up to?'

'What? Oh, never mind that,' he retorted dismissively, 'This is Lian,' he announced proudly, as though that was the only thing that mattered at the moment. 'She missed Dad at the station and started walking.'

'Well, thank goodness for that; I don't think poor Jared could have taken much more! He's already been back and forth like a demented shuttle.' With a warm smile, she extended her hand. 'Mary. Welcome to Bedlam.'

'Thank you, but——'

'And as for you, Simon,' she continued, 'you'd better go and get changed before your father sees you. He told you to stay clean!'

'Yes, I know, but there was this—— Uh-oh, hi, Dad.'

Swivelling back to the open doorway, Lian stared at the very large man standing behind Mary. A blown-up replica of his son with the same thick, untidy brown hair and dark brown eyes. What he didn't have was his son's air of friendly mischief. He looked restless, and decidedly irritable. He was dressed in a short-sleeved blue shirt and well-washed jeans—and he gave the impression of great power.

Subjecting her to a hard stare, he gave a nod, then flicked his eyes to his son. 'Go and get changed,' he ordered, 'you look disgraceful.'

'Yes, I know,' Simon agreed, not one whit subdued by the forceful manner, 'but Dad, this is Lian! Isn't she great? She missed you at the station...'

With a look of incredulity, the man stared back at Lian. 'You're from the agency?' he queried in disbelief.

'Yes, but I——'

'Great!' he exploded. 'That's really great! And where the hell have you been? No, don't answer that, I can see by your face that I probably won't like the answer. And didn't I *know* not to take someone sight unseen?' he demanded of himself. 'Yes, I bloody did!'

Totally astonished, and her gathering doubts over-ruled for the moment by his quite unfair criticism, Lian set her lips in a firm line. 'Now wait just a min-ute——'

'Why?' he demanded.

'Why?' she asked in confusion. 'Because you're being unfair, that's why.' Staring at him, taking in the pugnacious thrust of a very determined jaw, she in-vited, 'And just who are you to catechise me?'

'I——'

'And what on earth makes me so obviously un-suitable?' she interrupted with a little spurt of temper. 'Admittedly the agency didn't give me very many de-tails, only that I needed to be female, and able to drive, both of which apply, so what else is needed? Green hair? And it's hardly my fault if you've had to make several fruitless trips to the station to look for me, is it? I'm not responsible for British Rail's inefficiency.' Perhaps he hadn't wanted to pick her up, she mused, beginning to feel some of his own ob-vious irritation. Perhaps Mrs Popplewell had black-mailed him into it. And where on earth *was* Mrs Popplewell? 'Where is——?'

'Simon!' he thundered, his anger distracted mo-mentarily by his son, who had been gradually trying to edge away from the assembled group. 'Just where the hell do you think you're going?'

'Oh—er—nowhere...'

'Correct.' Giving him a look of disgusted resig-nation, the man indicated for him to come inside.

With a sheepish smile, Simon retraced his steps. He had one foot inside the back door before he was halted again.

'Shoes,' his father said neutrally.

Looking down, an expression of surprise crossed Simon's face, as though he couldn't for the life of him understand how they could have got in such a mess without him noticing. 'Oh, hell,' he muttered. 'Right.' Dragging them off by the heels on the metal foot-scraper beside the door, he gave a hopeful beam.

'And if that artless expression is supposed to divert me, let me tell you that it does nothing of the kind. I told you to stay clean.' Flicking his gaze back to Lian, he continued as though he hadn't been interrupted, 'So, Miss Hayes.'

'Hayes?' Lian queried in renewed confusion and the beginning of conviction. 'That's not my name.'

'Not?' he asked with some of the same confusion.

'No, it's Grayson.'

'What?'

'Grayson,' she repeated. 'And I think——'

'Oh, isn't that just typical?' he demanded of no one in particular. 'Not only do they send someone far too young, when I specifically asked for someone in her fifties, but they can't even get the name right! I do wonder, I really do wonder,' he muttered to himself as he retreated back through the kitchen, 'how some of these firms manage to exist. And make money!' The last barely audible as he disappeared from sight.

'Yes, but . . .' Exchanging a glance with Mary, who grinned, Lian queried lamely, 'Bedlam, did you say?'

'Yes. Don't take too much notice of Jared's behaviour; he's having a bad day. Back and forth to the station looking for you; phone calls that don't come. Ah, well, par for the course in this house. Now, where's your case?'

Staring at the friendly young woman before her, Lian gave a wry smile. 'Would you believe, at the station? But I'm——'

'Oh, lordy,' Mary grinned without allowing Lian to finish the sentence that she kept trying to insert, 'that means another trip. Oh, well, can't be helped, I suppose.' Switching her gaze to the boy, she crooked a finger at him. 'Come on, you; go and change, and on your way through show Miss Grayson where the study is before your father loses what little bit of temper he has left.'

Allowing herself to be shooed through the kitchen with Simon, as though they were geese, Lian philosophically decided that it might be better to sort it out with the irascible Jared than attempt to make Mary listen to her. She had allowed herself to be swept along by a beguiling child . . .

'Do you know anything about explosives?' Simon asked interestedly as he padded along beside her.

'Explosives? Good heavens, no!' she denied. 'Why?'

'Because Peter—that's a friend of mine—said you can use weed-killer——'

'Don't even try,' his father said from the open doorway on their right. 'Don't even think about trying. Miss Grayson, in here.'

'Yes, but——' Simon began.

'No.'

'Well, you were the one who said I had to have an enquiring mind,' the boy reproved indignantly. 'Had to find things out for myself! And if I couldn't find them in a book, you said, I was to ask. Well, what's the use of asking if no one will tell me the answer? Can I go out again?'

'Not if you're intending to experiment with weed-killer, no.'

'I wasn't,' he denied with a grin. 'Peter and me are making a——'

'I,' his father corrected. 'Peter and I.'

'Oh, right, well, we——'

'Simon,' his father interrupted with heavy patience, 'I am extremely short of time. I have to go into town; I have to interview Miss Grayson . . .'

'Oh, good. I'll stay, then.'

'You will not.'

'But it's for my benefit!' he exclaimed indignantly. 'I'm the one who'll have to put up with her . . .'

'Simon!' he thundered. 'How many times must I tell you to use people's names?'

'Sorry,' he mumbled, 'but——'

'No buts,' he interrupted. Turning to Lian, who was unsuccessfully trying to get a word in edgeways, he added, 'Now you will understand why I wanted an older woman.'

'Well, no . . .'

'You think you can control him?' Jared asked in disbelief. 'You think you can cope with the deplorable state he gets into? You——'

Unable to stand it any longer, Lian burst out, 'Mr—er——'

'Lowe,' he put in impatiently.

'Mr Lowe. There has obviously been some sort of mistake! I assumed, obviously wrongly, that your son was taking me to see Mrs Popplewell.'

'Mrs Pop—— Who the hell is Mrs Popplewell?'

'The woman I'm supposed to be working for!' she retorted in exasperation.

'The woman you're...? Then what the hell are you doing here?'

'I don't know!' she shouted.

Staring at her, Jared suddenly closed his eyes and slumped against the door-frame. 'I don't believe this. I really don't believe this.' Opening his eyes, he glared at her. 'Why in God's name couldn't you have said so before?'

'When?' she demanded. 'Every time I try to get a word in, I'm interrupted. Does no one ever get to finish a sentence in this house?'

'Don't be ridiculous! And you must have said something to Simon for him to think you were the woman we were waiting for!'

'No! Well, not intentionally,' she mumbled. 'I mean, I met him in the lane, and he just seemed to think——'

'*He* just seemed to think?' he asked incredulously. 'Didn't you even ask him?'

'Well, no...'

'Why?' he thundered.

'Because, well, because—oh, how the hell should I know? Presumably because he's as diverting as the rest of you!'

And how the devil did you explain to a man who clearly didn't want explanations that it had happened because you weren't thinking too straight right now? That you had taken the first job that came along because it didn't matter what it was, just that it would be something to do, something to divert your mind, stop you thinking about the might-have-beens? 'I stupidly assumed there couldn't be more than one idiot wandering around waiting to be interviewed, I suppose,' she concluded with a crotchety little twitch for her own stupidity.

'You suppose?' he exploded. 'You suppose? That's really intelligent, isn't it? And I do sometimes wonder just how the world came to be peopled with so many idiots!' With a grumpy sigh, he straightened, tried to look attentive. 'So what the hell do we do now? I needed someone *today*,' he burst out. 'Not tomorrow, not next week.'

'Dad,' Simon began hesitantly, giving a little tug on his father's leg to gain attention. 'Couldn't——?'

'What the devil are you still doing here? Go and get out of those wet things.'

'But Dad, we could——'

'No, we couldn't.' Extending his arm, Jared prodded his son backwards, drew Lian inside and closed the door. 'Now, sit,' he ordered, indicating a chair before a large, document-cluttered desk that held two half-buried telephones, she noticed, and what looked like a half-eaten sandwich.

'For what purpose?' she asked peevishly, but nevertheless doing as he said.

'For the purposes of deciding what to do.' Walking across the room, he seated himself behind the desk and leaned back. Glaring at her, he asked, 'Just who is this Mrs Popplewell?'

Unable to see the point of a discussion on the merits or otherwise of a woman he clearly didn't know, but deciding that sitting down did at least give her poor aching back a rest, Lian explained with as much patience as she could muster, 'A lady of independent means who wanted a female driver.'

'A driver?' he exclaimed. 'You're a driver?'

'Yes! And there is absolutely no need to sound so astonished,' she retorted pithily. 'Women do drive, you know.'

'I wasn't sounding astonished,' he denied irritably. 'I was sounding... Oh, I don't know what I was sounding,' he muttered defeatedly. 'Go on.'

Only too well aware of the fact that it was her own fault that she was in this ridiculous predicament, Lian put a determined brake on her temper. But if he continued to talk to her as though she were the same age as his son... 'The agency rang me last night,' she began quietly, 'told me Mrs P wanted a female driver, because she doesn't like men——'

'Well, she presumably married one!'

'Presumably she did!' she snapped. 'Which has nothing whatever to do with my explanation. Perhaps her husband ran off with the postmistress and she has now taken all men in aversion! I don't know. All I know is that she wanted a woman to drive her around to the various committees she sits on. That I was to be met at the station and taken to her house.' Shifting into a more comfortable position, suppressing her rising aggravation, she continued, 'There was no one to meet me—not surprising, seeing as the train was late—so I decided to walk; the rest you know. And I can only assume that the Miss Hayes you were obviously expecting did likewise...'

'And also got lost?' he asked with sarcastic helpfulness.

'No,' she denied through teeth that were beginning to grit, 'but I'm beginning to wonder if there hasn't been some sort of mix-up and she's gone to Mrs Popplewell in my stead.'

'Did anyone else get off the train with you?'

'Not to my knowledge.'

'Well, then,' he pronounced as though it were all her fault that the woman had somehow become mislaid.

'Well, then, what?' she exclaimed. 'Just because I didn't see her doesn't mean she wasn't there!'

'True.'

'Or perhaps she missed it.'

'Perhaps, although it seems extremely odd that there should be two of you needing to be picked up from the same station, at the same time. And both from an agency.'

'Odd or not, that appears to be what has happened, so I would be extremely grateful if you would now let me return to that same station!'

'And hope Miss Hayes turns up, I suppose?' he derided.

'Well, I'm not responsible for her!'

'I didn't say you were. But it—— Oh, for God's sake,' he muttered as a telephone began ringing shrilly. Irritably scattering papers, he unearthed it and snatched up the receiver. 'Yes?' he barked. 'What? No, no, thank you.' Replacing it, he stared somewhat blankly at her for a minute. 'Where were we? Oh, yes, Miss Hayes, a prospective housekeeper. Someone to keep an eye on that hell-born brat out there.'

'Ah!' she exclaimed softly as she recalled Simon's words.

'Ah?' he queried with a scowl.

'He seemed to take some pride in the fact that no one ever stayed very long.'

'Oh. They don't,' he admitted, his tone slightly more conciliatory. Staring at her, he gave a twisted grimace. 'And I suppose that little gleam in your eye is because you think you can quite understand why.'

'Well, would you,' she demanded, 'if the positions were reversed? I don't think I have ever come across a more confusing family.'

'Then you must have led a very sheltered life.'

Sheltered? No, but she sometimes thought it might have been better if she had. A sadness in her beautiful eyes, she stared at the strong face opposite, then gave a reluctant smile when he poked irritably at the half-eaten sandwich. He looked like a thwarted little boy. 'Oh, do stop scowling,' she reproved. 'Laying blame won't solve anything.'

'No,' he agreed moodily, then, much to her surprise, he gave her an extraordinarily captivating smile, even if it did hold a touch of calculation. 'Why don't we start again?'

Not being a fool, Lian could see very clearly where his thoughts were heading, and it was most definitely a direction she didn't want to go. 'No,' she denied softly.

'No? Why not? It would temporarily solve both our problems,' Jared said rather arrogantly. 'I know we started off on the wrong foot, but surely we can at least discuss it? I'm quite willing to apologise—if you will,' he tacked on provokingly.

'How very handsome of you,' she approved with a sweet little smile. 'However, I have nothing to apologise for!'

'You don't? Interviewees aren't usually conciliatory?' he queried with a humour that crinkled his eyes and smoothed out the harsh lines of his face.

'I am not an interviewee,' she pointed out, 'I'm a——'

'Mistaken identity?' he asked helpfully. 'But you didn't know that when we met at the back door. Did you?'

'Beginning to suspect,' she put in.

'Which was why you were looking so frosty-faced?' he queried lightly.

'Possibly—and of course the fact that no one would let me say what I was trying to say.'

'Mm,' he agreed ruefully. 'A case of our mouths jumping ahead of our thoughts. I was also unbearably irritated. I'd been back and forth to the station, afraid of missing you, afraid of missing a very important telephone call... It has, Miss Grayson, been one hell of a day.'

'Yes. And the answer is still no.'

With a smile that appeared much more genuine, albeit reluctant, Jared agreed, 'Oh, all right, if you won't, you won't, and I can't say I honestly blame you. What time does this agency of yours close?'

'Five.'

Glancing at his watch, seeing it was five-thirty, he sighed. 'Where do you have to get back to?'

'Ah, yes, back to,' she echoed, then did a little cursing of her own. 'Oh, well, I can probably dump myself on a friend for the night.'

'Meaning?'

'Meaning I sublet my flat for the next four weeks.'

'Bit hasty, wasn't it?' he asked in surprise. 'You might not have liked the job.'

'True. However, I had agreed to give it a month's trial. In which case, I wouldn't need my flat, would I? If I liked it, I'd stay; if I didn't, I'd leave at the end of the allotted period and return home.'

'Still doesn't seem a very intelligent thing to have done; however, it's none of my business.'

'No,' Lian agreed. 'It isn't.'

With a grunt of laughter, he asked, 'What was it, man trouble?'

'No,' she denied tightly, because it wasn't, or not entirely. Neither was it any of his business. 'So, if you would kindly direct me to the station?'

'Or Mrs Popplewell? If we can find her, that is.'

'And do a swap?'

'Mm, sounds logical, don't you think?'

'Very,' she agreed in a dry little voice.

'Good. And why my life has to get so complicated, I will never understand.'

While he searched for, and finally unearthed, the local directory from a pile of books stacked on the floor, and began to hunt through the Ps, she watched him. He had a strong face, a very attractive face, and he looked like a man who knew where he was going— and how to get what he wanted when he got there.

'No Popplewell,' he grunted, slamming the book shut. Picking up the phone, he tried Directory Enquiries, again without success. Replacing the receiver, he leaned back in his chair. Chewing on his lower lip, he gazed off into space.

Still watching him, knowing exactly what was coming next, Lian gave a derisive smile when he asked artfully, 'Can you cook?'

'No. Neither do I wish to learn, and, if you're thinking what I think you're thinking, don't.'

'Simon likes you . . .'

'The answer is still no.'

Steepling his fingers under his chin, Jared gave a frustrated sigh. 'Why?' he queried. 'Pride? Doesn't fit in with the image you have of yourself?'

'I don't have an image of myself,' she denied smoothly. 'Neither has it anything to do with pride. What it has to do with,' she informed him kindly, 'is the fact that I thoroughly dislike domestic pursuits.'

'Oh.' He looked nonplussed for a moment, then brightened. 'What about temporarily keeping an eye on a boy who seems determined to see me into an early grave?'

'No good,' she told him sorrowfully. 'I can't climb trees, and you're straw-clutching.'

'Well, of course I am! Wouldn't you? Just for to-night?' he pleaded. 'I mean, you don't have anything better to do, do you?'

'No.'

'Well, then. And that school-marm air of yours might be very effective. It sure as hell is cowing me!'

'That I very much doubt, and I do *not* have a school-marm air!' she denied on a reluctant laugh.

'No?' he queried lightly, one eyebrow raised. 'Well, whatever, I can't and *won't* keep relying on Mary. It isn't fair. She has her own family to care for.' Glancing at his watch again, Jared groaned. 'I have a meeting in an hour, and I haven't even *glanced* through the damned papers.'

'Then I'd best be going and leave you to get on with it.' Suppressing her smile, and the teasing laughter in her eyes that was so very much like the old Lian, the girl she had been before a set of unforeseen circumstances changed her life forever, she began to get up.

'You couldn't!' he reproved. 'Could you?'

'Probably not,' she said wryly, and found to her surprise that she was actually enjoying herself—and had actually made a conscious note of the fact that there didn't seem to be a wife around. Or maybe she was just away on a trip. And why on earth should that disappoint her? She didn't even *know* the man. Shaking her head at her own foolishness, she settled back in the chair. 'Do people always do your bidding, I wonder?' she asked in some amusement.

Looking astonished for a moment, as though he either didn't understand the question, or why anyone would query it, he suddenly grinned. 'Yes. Always.'

That Lian did believe, and for a fleeting moment his charm, his cajoling reminded her of David, and her smile died. He'd been nice to her, wooed her in order to get his own way—in his case gain entry into a world he coveted, her world, the world of yachting— and when his goal had been attained he'd dropped her, because she'd been of no further use. Was this another man who used his charm to ruthlessly get his own way? It certainly looked like it, but his manipulation would suit her own ends too, wouldn't it? As he had truthfully said, she had nothing better to do. What difference would one night spent here make? None, and she didn't really want to trail all the way back to Southampton, did she?

Flicking her wide grey eyes back to his face, she smiled at his hopeful expression, and, if her smile was just a little bit cynical, then he would have to make of it what he would. Normally very positive, she was getting decidedly fed up with a day sadly lacking in it. 'Very well, one night. You need someone to feed Simon and keep an eye on him while you are at your meeting. Yes?'

'Yes!' he agreed fervently.

'Right. Despite being lacking in the culinary arts, I can probably rustle up a snack of some sort.'

'Mm, or,' he murmured thoughtfully, 'if I haven't finished going through my papers by the time I need to leave for the meeting, you could drive me to it and I could finish them off in the back of the car.'

'Providing the car is an automatic,' she qualified.

'It is. Can't drive a manual?' he asked curiously.

Tempted to say no, Lian gave a little sigh, and confessed, 'Not at the moment.' She might have known, mightn't she, that he wouldn't leave it there?

'Why?'

'Back injury,' she said shortly.

'Which makes depressing a clutch difficult?'

'Yes.'

'And climbing trees?' he added with a gentle smile.

'Yes,' she agreed.

'All right, so if we go in the car Simon could come with us...'

'And while you're in the meeting I could take him for a burger.'

Leaning back in his chair, Jared grinned. 'Now you've caught it.'

Puzzled, she asked, 'What?'

'Not allowing anyone to finish a sentence.'

Mentally reviewing the last conversation, she gave a faint smile. 'Oh, sorry.'

'No problem. So, you want to stay here the night? Or find a hotel?'

'I don't mind,' she admitted, then, with a rueful smile, confessed, 'The only trouble is, my suitcase is at the station.'

Eyeing her for a moment, he slumped in mock defeat. 'Well, it would be, wouldn't it?' Leaning sideways, he rummaged in his pocket and produced some keys. Dangling them in front of her, he waited.

'Fetch it myself, right?'

'Right.'

With a wry smile, she took them. 'OK, I'll see you later. How long have I got before you need to leave?'

'Half an hour.'

Nodding, she got stiffly to her feet and walked out. She did not see his amused smile. Which was probably just as well.

Simon was sitting on the stairs, having clearly been listening. 'Find it interesting, did you?' she teased.

'Terrific,' he enthused cheekily. 'But I don't like burgers. Chinese?' he asked hopefully.

'Very well,' she agreed. 'Now go and change.'

'Don't you want me to come with you to the station?'

'Oh, I'm sure I can find it,' she said drily.

With a laugh, he scrambled to his feet and went upstairs obediently.

As she drove to the station, Lian wondered again about the wife and mother. Dead? Divorced? None of your business, Lian, she scolded herself. True, but to date they seemed the sort of family that dragged you willy-nilly into their business whether you wanted to be dragged or not, so they could hardly expect her not to be curious, could they?

Collecting her case, she returned to the house where she was met again by Mary, who showed her to the room she would be using before hurrying off to take care of her own family. The bedroom was large, comfortable, and spotlessly clean. There was also, she

discovered to her relief, an en-suite bathroom.
Unfortunately, there would be no time to have a nice
hot bath, which was something she most definitely
yearned for to ease the abominable ache in her back.
Her own fault, of course; the doctor had told her not
to walk too far at first, so what had she done? Walked
at least three miles looking for Mrs P, instead of
waiting at the station like a good little girl.

With a sour grimace, she awkwardly hoisted her
case on to the ottoman at the foot of the bed, and
silently cursed the limitations which her injured back
now put on her. Once upon a time she could have
slung it around without thought; now she must constantly remind herself of what she must not do.
Suppressing a sigh, she opened it and took out clean
clothes. With the dogged determination that had seen
her through the past few traumatic weeks, she walked
into the bathroom.

Stripping off, she had a quick wash, then dressed
in clean underwear, tailored grey trousers and a rather
masculine grey shirt which only emphasised her look
of fragility. Yet her lean body had a whipcord
strength, a toughness belied by her obvious femi-
ninity. Or it had, she thought with a brief return to
bitterness. Knotting a pink and grey silk scarf at her
neck, she tidied her hair, renewed her make-up, pushed
her feet into flat black shoes, picked up her soft leather
bag, and stiffened her resolve. Time to stop being an
observer. Time to participate. Rejoin the human race.
So you've had a raw deal; so have a lot of other
people, and crying about it won't make it change,
won't put it back to how it was.

No, but telling herself, and actually doing it, were
two entirely different things, as she had discovered all

too frequently of late. And yet today, meeting Simon and his decidedly provocative father, she had actually felt quite cheerful, had managed to forget her own troubles—because, of course, they didn't know of them, and therefore could not remind her of her loss.

And that was such a relief, she admitted, after the stilted conversations with her own friends, who were all from the world of yachting. There had been embarrassment and awkwardness when they'd visited her in the hospital, with no one knowing quite what to say, as though she had a terminal illness. It had probably been a relief to all concerned when she had been discharged and moved away from the area. She had given them a determinedly bright smile, wished them luck in their racing, and promised to write. And yet cutting herself off from all that she had known and loved was beginning to seem just as much a punishment as staying had been. She missed the sound of the sea; the constant bustle of the quayside; the warmth of seeing familiar faces. With a long sigh, she opened the bedroom door.

Her reluctant, and very temporary employer was emerging from a room along the landing as she emerged from hers. He had changed into a navy suit, and looked as though he hated wearing it. He was too rugged-looking for formality, Lian decided. Too impatient for a restrictive collar and tie, and then was surprised at herself for noticing, because noticing things belonged to the old Lian, not this new stranger she was trying so desperately to come to terms with.

Unaware that she had been staring, she only gradually became aware of the long, comprehensive glance he was giving her. His lips twitched infinitesimally when she blinked and gave him a small, meaningless smile, and then he gave an approving nod. At least, Lian preferred to think of it as approving; it was probably nothing of the sort.

'Very businesslike,' he murmured. 'Ready?'

'Yes.'

'Good. Simon?' he yelled.

'Coming!'

Simon erupted out of his room as though he'd been on the blocks waiting for the starter's pistol. Presenting himself in front of his father, presumably for approval, he grinned, and winked at Lian.

Their noisy progress to the car, as they argued amiably about some topic or another, she found amusing, which again surprised her. She liked order, reason, so it was quite extraordinary that she should be diverted, rather than irritated, by the continual bickering that had gone on in this house since she had arrived.

Simon elected to sit in the front, ostensibly to direct her into the small market town and the office where his father was to have his meeting. In reality, it seemed, it was to interrogate her on her lifestyle; her thoughts on this or that; her preferences in music, sport, and any other subject that his fertile brain could come up with. His father might be looking at his papers, but Lian got the distinct impression that they held only half his attention, and that the other half was on how she answered or fielded his son's questions.

If it was a test, she wondered if she ought to point out that she had no interest in either passing or failing, although perhaps that was why—because she was not trying to impress anyone—she inadvertently struck the right note. Neither patronising nor gushing, she answered those questions that she could calmly, comprehensibly. To those she couldn't, she confessed ignorance, without excuse. Questions that bordered on the personal, she did not answer at all.

When they reached their destination, Lian halted the car, but left the engine running. Collecting his papers together, Jared got out.

'Thanks,' he said absently. 'Where will you be?'

'The nearest Chinese restaurant.'

'Hung's House,' he said with a nod. 'You'll be able to park outside. If I finish first, I'll come and find you. If not, come back here and wait.' Bending slightly, he fixed his son with a gimlet eye. 'Behave,' he warned him.

'Sure,' Simon grinned. 'Don't I always? Want us to get you a take-away?'

With a little shudder, he politely refused. Straightening, he nodded to Lian, took a deep breath as though a fight was imminent, and strode into the building.

Curbing her curiosity, Lian glanced at her youthful companion. 'OK,' she said easily. 'Where to?'

She didn't know much about small boys, didn't *know* any other small boys, so she treated him much as she would have done an adult and allowed him free rein to choose what he liked.

He was old enough to know what he wanted, she decided, old enough to make his own mistakes, and, if he chose wrongly, well, next time he would know better. She also, much to her surprise, continued to find him an amusing and diverting companion. In fact, all in all, it had been a thoroughly diverting day, and it was showing her a side of herself she hadn't known existed. With a little frown, she actually wondered, for the first time in her life, if she hadn't been missing out on something while she had been single-mindedly pursuing her love of yachting.

'So that was how I got in such a mess,' Simon explained with a wide grin.

Hastily dragging her attention back, she gave what she hoped was an understanding smile, and one that didn't let him know that she hadn't heard what he said. Taking a sip of her mineral water, she encouraged him to talk, and this time listened while he chattered about his interests, school, what he hoped to do in the holidays, yet never once did he mention his mother. Neither did he say anything about his father, the business he was in, the meeting. Nothing in fact that his father might take exception to. Because he had been warned?

When they had finished, and with still no sign of his father, they drove back to the centre of town. Parking outside the building, they waited less than five minutes before he came striding out, his face grim. There was a tight line round his mouth, and both she and Simon were warned. Don't ask questions. Not that Lian had intended to. Resentful of questions about herself, she would not have dreamed of prying into anyone else's life. Even if she was interested. Which she wasn't, she assured herself.

They drove back to the house in silence. Simon, with a brief goodnight to them both, went up to bed. His father went into his study and closed the door. Lian went to the kitchen and made herself a cup of tea. Not her place to ask anything. Not her place to offer. Because she would be leaving in the morning? Because she didn't want to get involved any further in this curiously likeable family? Taking her tea up to her room, she sat in the comfortable armchair by the window. So why on earth did she feel guilty that she had not even offered him a cup of tea?

Early rising had been part of her life for so long that her internal clock woke her at six. She lay for a while, thinking her own thoughts, recalling the events of yesterday. Knowing she would not get back to sleep, she then rose, showered, and, with the forthcoming meeting with Mrs Popplewell in mind, dressed in a neat grey skirt and white silk blouse. Carefully making up her face and brushing her brown wavy hair until it shone, she tied it back from her face with a silk scarf and went down to the kitchen. The pain in her back had, thankfully, settled down to a minor niggle.

Expecting to be the only one up, she was a little disconcerted to find her temporary employer sitting at the kitchen table, a cup of tea nursed in his strong hands. Obviously showered and shaved, he was dressed again in jeans and a check shirt.

'Good morning, Mr Lowe,' she greeted quietly.

Looking up, his eyes blank for a moment, as though he had been pondering some weighty matter, he finally nodded.

'Morning. And it's Jared. Mr Lowe makes me sound like my father. You're up early.'

'Yes. Is there tea in the pot?'

'Sure. Help yourself.' Leaning back in his chair, he watched her, watched the neat, economic movements that she made, and when she came to sit opposite him he asked abruptly, 'How keen are you to work for this Mrs Popplewell?'

'Oh, not again,' she reproved with an exasperated smile.

'Yes, again. Think about it,' he ordered.

Leaning back in her chair, Lian eyed him somewhat sardonically for a moment before doing as he had asked, and then, with an intriguing little gleam of humour in her lovely eyes, she informed him quietly, 'I am keen to work—no, that's not strictly true; I need to work. As a driver,' she qualified specifically. 'Mrs Popplewell is an unknown quantity, so I don't know if I'm keen to work for her in particular. Does that answer your question?'

'Mm, I suppose so.' He looked amused. Because she was being pedantic? Continuing to stare at her as though weighing up pros and cons, he finally said, 'Due to recent circumstances that I won't go into, it's possible that I'll need a driver. There will be a great many meetings I will need to attend, which means paperwork, and, due to the turmoil which usually reigns in this household, it's not always easy to work here undisturbed.' Faint humour appeared in his dark eyes, and he added, 'Your suggestion of working in the back of the car...'

'My suggestion?' she queried blandly.

'Made a great deal of sense,' he continued determinedly, 'but before I ask if you would consider working for me, and you tell me whether you would even entertain the idea, I need to ask you some questions.'

'Very well,' she said composedly, 'but before you do I should perhaps point out that I still have no desire to work in a house that is ruled by chaos.'

A faint twitch to his lips, Jared looked down. 'It isn't always,' he denied. 'Turmoil, yes, but the chaos stems from a set of circumstances that are now, hopefully, nearly at an end.' Glancing back up, he asked with even more obvious amusement, 'May I continue?'

'By all means.'

'You have, to date, apart from our earlier misunderstandings, been very quiet. Are you usually?'

Quiet? Once upon a time that wouldn't have been true of her. But now? Oh, yes, this new Lian could be very quiet. 'I don't chatter, if that's what you mean.'

'It is. Secondly, I was listening when you were talking to my son. I was impressed. You're quite clearly very intelligent. Driving a car does not take a great deal, so I would like to ask why you do it?'

Not bothering to take issue on the back-handed compliment, and not wishing to go into a lot of explanations that could be of no possible interest to him—and because they would also be painful to herself—she replied quietly, 'Because I can. No, let me finish,' she added quickly as he looked in imminent danger of apoplexy. 'I drive because that, at the moment, is all I can think of to do...'

'Because of your back,' he put in with an understanding nod.

'Yes. I was trained by my father, an ex-police instructor, which means that I am very good at it. I have a clean licence, no criminal record——'

'And if that, Miss Grayson, is intended as a putdown, or to divert me from asking other, more intimate questions, like what is it you did before, and can now no longer do, let me assure you that it does no such thing. It merely piques my interest.'

'Then your interest,' she replied as lightly as she could, 'will have to remain piqued, because that is as much information as I am prepared to give.'

'Hm. How old are you?'

'Twenty-eight. How old are you?'

'Thirty-seven.' Shaking his head, Jared gave a little chuckle, and the attraction that Lian had felt the day before was redoubled, and that was odd, because it wasn't a dispassionate feeling. Ever since the accident that had robbed her of her life's ambition she had become used to looking at life through a haze, of nothing very much mattering, and yet now, suddenly, here she was, feeling attracted to this very strong-looking man. He seemed tough, dependable, a man who was comfortable with his own masculinity. Someone who had nothing to prove. She liked that about him. Unpretentious herself, it was something that she admired in others. But that did not mean she was prepared to trust him wholly, or take his words at face value, because, as with David, self-interest seemed to be his motivating force.

Taking her by surprise, he reached across the table and picked up her hand. He inspected the short nails, turned it over and stared at the palm, then looked up at her. Holding her gaze while his thumb explored the hard, ridged skin, he teased, 'Manual work?'

'Messing about in boats,' she corrected glibly.

With a whimsical smile, he observed, 'You're a long way from the sea.'

'Yes.'

'Don't want to do it any more?' he probed.

'God, but you're determined!' she reproved in exasperation.

'Yes. So?'

'*Can't* do it any more,' she said flatly, 'because of my back, remember?'

'I always remember,' he told her simply, 'which means you hurt it rather more badly than you led me to believe. What did you do?'

Her face stiff, she said shortly, 'Tore some ligaments, damaged vertebrae, and spent two weeks in hospital flat on my back. They tried a bit of stretching, a bit of physiotherapy...'

'And then sent you on your way and told you to be careful.'

'Correct. Can we now drop the subject?'

With an affable nod, he released her hand and picked up his cup again. 'What time does the agency open?'

'Eight-thirty.' Profoundly relieved by his easy acceptance of her desire to change the subject, Lian glanced at the kitchen clock. 'Almost seven-thirty,' she murmured. 'Another hour.'

'Time for breakfast. I suddenly find that I'm hungry. You?'

'Yes,' she agreed with an intriguing little air of amazement. 'Yes, I rather think I am.' Another surprise—she hadn't felt hungry for weeks.

'Then you sit there and drink your tea, and I will demonstrate my hard-learned culinary skills.'

While he fried bacon, bread and eggs, she watched him. A confusing and likeable man, she decided, and in the space of twenty-four hours he had learned a great deal more about her than she had about him. And if he had no qualms about probing into someone else's life... 'Is your wife away?' she asked quietly.

'You might say so.' With a brief glance over his shoulder, his face oddly closed, he added quietly, 'She's dead.'

'Oh, I'm sorry.' And the subject was now closed? she wondered. His shuttered face had certainly given that impression. Because it had been recent? More than usually traumatic? Did that account for the fact that there were no pictures of her around? And if it had been recent it would be the height of insensitivity to pursue it, and Lian was anything but insensitive. Also, despite his pleasant, mostly friendly air, there was an underlying reserve to his manner, and she got the feeling that any attempt to get past the barrier would result in the shutters being very firmly closed. There was to be no prying into his life. Why, when he obviously had no qualms about prying into hers? 'Don't practise what you preach, do you?' she asked softly.

'Mm?'

'You pry into my life, yet I'm firmly repulsed when I try to do the same.'

With an amused sideways glance, he observed, 'Life just ain't fair sometimes, is it?'

'No,' she agreed wryly, and it wasn't, because she would have liked to know about his life. Whether he'd been desperately in love with his wife. Whether he was sad without her. He didn't look sad. He looked . . . complete. He was quick-tempered, as she knew from the day before. He didn't like deceit, or sham—at least, she assumed he didn't, from what he had said previously, yet he had been amused rather than angry by her own evasion a short time ago. There was an obvious close bond between himself and his son.

Lian didn't know if she could trust him, but she definitely liked him, and, against her will, she was beginning to be extremely intrigued. 'Don't look inwards, darling,' her father had told her after the accident. 'Look outwards, see what's going on around you. Look at it through different eyes.' Well, she was trying. Some days were harder than others, but she was trying. And since she'd met this confusing family it seemed to be working.

Her introspection was cut short by the arrival of Simon. 'Good heavens!' his father exclaimed.

Turning to grin at Lian, the boy explained with an adult air that was rather comical, 'He means, I am up and dressed ...'

'And hopefully washed,' his father put in.

'Dressed,' Simon continued determinedly, 'without being shouted at!'

'Sit,' his father commanded. Putting the first breakfast before his son, he turned back to cook Lian's and then his own. They had barely finished when there came a thunderous knocking on the door. 'Oh, hell, who's that at this hour?'

While Jared went to open the door, and Simon to follow, and hover curiously, Lian cleared away the breakfast dishes and stacked them in the dishwasher. Putting the kettle on to make more tea, she turned in surprise when Simon stormed back into the kitchen, his face set in a scowl. Halting in front of the table, he addressed the scrubbed wood with a great deal of belligerence. 'I'm not having her!'

'Who?'

Turning to look at her, his expression very reminiscent of his father, he stated unequivocally, 'Her! Miss Hayes. And I'm not having her, so he needn't think I am!'

'Keep your voice down, you revolting brat,' Jared said quietly as he slipped into the kitchen.

'I'm not ha——'

'I already heard you,' his father reproved.

'She smells!' Simon stated as though that was the clincher to any argument that might ensue. 'And she'd better not be here when I get home from school!' he warned grimly. Grabbing up his satchel from the floor where he had flung it earlier, he stalked out.

Turning to look at Jared, a rather bewildered amusement in her eyes, Lian asked, 'Does she?'

Staring at her, a look of indecision on his face, as though he was debating whether gentlemanly conduct would allow him to agree, or deny it, Jared's eyes suddenly filled with devilish laughter. 'Yes, and he's quite right—she won't do. He'd run rings round her in seconds.'

'Did she get the day wrong?'

'No, you were right, there was a mix-up, and she went to Mrs Popplewell. She apparently arrived there yesterday in time to ring the agency when she discovered the mistake. Spent the night in a local hotel, and came along here this morning.'

'And is now returning whence she came,' Lian murmured with a teasing smile.

'Mm. Will you run her to the station?'

'Yes, of course, and if you'll allow me further use of the car I'll get Mrs Popplewell's address from her, and go and see her on the way back.'

'Does that mean you've decided to work for me?' he queried hopefully.

'No, it means I've decided to go and see Mrs Popplewell. However, if I don't like her...' Taking the car keys he held out, Lian went to find Miss Hayes. There was a little smile playing about her mouth, a twinkle of amusement in her lovely eyes.

CHAPTER TWO

As soon as Lian met Mrs Popplewell, no decision was needed. Forget grey-haired old lady, forget apples, unless they were the crab variety. Mrs Popplewell, or Vera, as she told Lian she preferred to be called, was Attila the Hun in drag. With profuse apologies for any disruption, Lian fled back to Jared Lowe and the comfort of Bedlam.

He greeted her return with a little bow. 'I rang the agency,' he told her solemnly. 'And told them that you would be working for me for a while.'

'Did you indeed? Bit premature, wasn't it?'

'Decisive,' he argued. 'I assumed you would approve—being so decisive yourself.'

'Hm. And I would suggest, meekly of course, that you remove your tongue from your cheek before you accidentally bite it.' Walking past him, she placed the car keys carefully on the hall bureau. 'Did the agency say how the mix-up occurred?'

'They did. The details of employment you were both given were correct in all things but address.'

'Oh.'

'I also,' he added as he followed her into the kitchen, 'asked them to send further candidates for the post of housekeeper.'

'Good.'

'Cup of tea?' he asked, only the suspicion of a quiver in his voice.

'Please.'

38

When he had made and poured the tea, he joined her at the table. 'So, you will work for me?'

'I will *drive* for you,' Lian emphasised.

A look of satisfaction on his strong face, Jared unfolded the piece of paper that lay in front of him, and passed it across. 'I've made a list of the meetings I'll need to attend this week. Times, addresses, probable length. Until I can get this business of a housekeeper sorted out I've been trying to get back here in time for Simon's return from school each afternoon. It's a damned nuisance, but I'm not letting him loose on the community without supervision; the Lord only knows what he'll get up to.'

'He's very bright...'

'Substitute that for inventive and I might agree with you,' he said drily. 'And he'll either turn out to be brilliant—the head of whichever field he chooses to go into—or a criminal. At the moment criminal has the edge. But I'm unbelievably proud of him,' he added softly, 'and have to confess to a sneaking admiration for his prowess. And somewhere, please God, there is a housekeeper who will be able to cope with him.'

'How long have you been looking?'

'A year,' he admitted mournfully. 'There have been an army of temporary ones, all of whom my son has taken in dislike. Two were possibles, who actually stayed for more than a week, but for one reason or another eventually decided they couldn't cope with him. Or me,' he added, and although there was a faint twinkle in his dark eyes they also held a warning. Even more intriguing; what was she being warned against? she wondered.

'He has to have someone he can respect,' Jared continued, obviously unaware of her thoughts, 'someone he will obey, or at least listen to. Someone motherly. He might look tough, confident, but inside ... inside there's a little boy who doesn't know what the hell he's doing, or why.'

Touched against her will by what he had said, Lian looked down into her tea. Don't get too involved, she warned herself, this is only temporary. Next week you might find yourself working for someone else.

'Sorry,' he apologised. 'Not your concern. I have a lot on my mind at the moment, and sometimes it's nice to have someone to talk to. Nice to—share.'

Surprised, because Jared didn't look the sort of man who needed the approval of others, she gave a wry grin when he elaborated.

'To discuss my son, I meant. Teachers don't count, because they tend not to see him as I do, so a little bit of feminine input can be important. You seem to have struck up quite a rapport with him, and for that I'm unbelievably grateful.'

'I don't know about rapport,' she denied with some amusement. 'I think it's more a case of him thinking he can twist me round his little finger. Which he probably can,' she added ruefully.

Over the next few days she became convinced of it; she didn't think she had ever met a child who could get into so much trouble so quickly. Or have the most amazing reasons for doing so. You'd have to be awake on every suit to even get close! He could also, if he thought it worth the effort, charm his way past the veriest cynic. Like his father, who now that he had charmed his way past her defences wasn't bothering to be charming any more. Although that was probably unfair; he obviously had a lot on his mind, and she didn't think his lack of charm was a conscious thing, just the need to devote all his energies to his business. Whatever that was—but certainly his outbursts seemed to stem from frustration, and weren't intended as a personal attack on herself, or anyone else who happened to be in the line of fire.

And not only was there the need to keep an eye on his son, but to find time to look for a housekeeper—time he clearly didn't have, and without really thinking about it Lian began to devise ways of helping him, take some of the load from his shoulders.

She had even, much to her inward amusement, learned how to use the fax machine in his study, how to switch on the word processor and print out stored information. Not that it seemed to be appreciated, she thought wryly, yet instead of being annoyed by the cutting remarks he made, by the change from warm, friendly and confiding to monosyllabic, contained, and tight-lipped, she felt only challenge, and sympathy. Which was extremely odd.

She had gathered that he was the owner of a large engineering works, but not what the trouble was that was causing him so much frustration. The furious round of meetings to which she drove him were with lawyers, his bank, and obviously important customers. He also had a secretary, who sometimes joined him in the rear of the car, and who also seemed to come in for her fair share of being shouted at; yet instead of it forging a bond with Lian it seemed to have the opposite effect. The woman would sometimes look at Lian with a dislike that bordered on hatred. Why? She was twenty-four maybe, attractive, with short dark hair and blue eyes, and for some reason she seemed very proprietorial towards Jared. Or she seemed very proprietorial towards him when she knew Lian was watching. Because she thought Lian a threat?

Instead of being amused, which she should have been, Lian was somewhat horrified to discover that she felt a bit proprietorial towards him herself. Not jealousy, of course, more a desire that he should have someone nicer—as his secretary. Yes, that was all it was, and that was why she began to watch them when they were together. Speculate about whether they were personally involved with each other. Anyway, it took her mind off her own troubles, didn't it?

She also discovered, to add to those troubles, that driving, as an occupation, was not for her. The constant sitting in one position made her injured back ache abominably—as the doctor had warned her, she conceded wryly, but which her stubborn pride had made her at least try—and she had finally, after much soul-searching, come to the conclusion that it would be best to put her flat up for sale and move down to Devon to stay with her father until she could find another niche for herself. Depriving herself of the sight and sound of the sea *had* been a mistake. She missed it damnably.

Catching a movement from the corner of her eye, she turned to see the office door opening. Jared strode out and climbed into the back of the car without a word. He looked tired, and thoroughly fed up. His tie was wrenched down, his top button undone, his hair untidy, as though he had been thrusting his hands through it. Someone else with too many troubles. Putting the car in drive, Lian moved smoothly away, and when they arrived back at the house it was to find yet another prospective housekeeper waiting for him. Mary had let her in and put her in his study to wait. With a long sigh, Jared went to interview her.

Walking into the lounge, where Simon was hunched dejectedly in an armchair watching the television, Lian thankfully eased herself down into the chair opposite.

'What's this one like?' she asked gently.

'Awful,' he said gloomily. 'She called me a little boy.'

'Oh,' Lian commented.

'Well, you never do!' he retorted.

'No. I have more sense,' she teased.

'I wish Nan hadn't died,' he added quietly.

'Nan?'

'She came after Mum died,' he explained quietly. 'When I was two. She died last year. She was nice.' Fixing his eyes firmly on the flickering screen, he pretended absorption.

Understanding that the subject was still too painful for him to talk about, Lian picked up the newspaper from the table beside her chair, not because she wanted to read it, but as a shield for her thoughts. His mother had died seven years ago? A long time for Jared to be grieving still ... Or wasn't it grieving? Yet what other reason could there be for his refusal to discuss her? Lian had assumed, obviously wrongly, that her death had been recent. Unusual, too, that such an attractive man, especially one with a young son, had not remarried. Was that how Heather felt? And would like very much to be the next Mrs Lowe?

Pulling a face of disgust at her preoccupation with something that was none of her business, Lian focused her eyes on the newsprint and attempted to distract her thoughts. She very carefully avoided glancing at anything to do with sport, in case yachting was mentioned.

Ten minutes later she heard the front door close. Another one bit the dust? When Jared walked into the lounge, she saw the effort he made to suppress his own problems in order to behave naturally with his son.

'All right, Simon, you can take that look off your face,' he said tiredly. 'She's gone.'

'She wasn't any good,' he muttered.

'I know.'

'I don't know why I need one anyway. I'm nearly ten.'

'In eleven months, yes,' his father agreed.

Leaning moodily back in his chair, Simon eyed his father. 'Why can't I have Lian?' he asked as though it was something he'd only just thought of. Only Lian got the definite feeling that it was something he'd been thinking about for some time, and had mentioned before.

'Because she doesn't want to be a housekeeper, and because she's acting as my chauffeur,' Jared said with the patience of a man who had indeed been all through this before.

'You could drive yourself,' the boy muttered.

'Could,' Jared agreed. 'But won't. At the moment I need that time in the car to prepare for meetings.'

Two strong-willed males, Lian thought, as she stared from one to the other. Father and son, alike as two peas in a pod. Look at the boy, and you saw the man as he had once been, and she finally consciously admitted that she felt for them both. Really cared for them both. Cared what happened to them, and that was worrying, because she really didn't want

to get involved with anyone else. Not yet, not so soon
after David. She was still vulnerable from that let-
down, still emotionally unstable. 'What?' she asked
blankly as she finally registered that Simon was talking
to her.

'I said you like looking after me, don't you? You
said so.'

'I said I liked you,' she corrected, 'and I do,
but——'

'Then why can't Dad get another chauffeur?' he
insisted. 'He could have one of the women he keeps
trying to foist off on me.'

'Foist?' his father asked softly. 'Define foist.'

With a smug smile, which only partly hid his inner
turmoil, Simon explained triumphantly, 'Make have.
Fob off on.'

Jared was just unable to stop the faint twitch of his
lips in time. 'Been at the dictionary, I see. Well, I
can't complain at that, can I?'

'No.'

'And if you become too sharp you'll cut yourself.'

Still eyeing his father, as though trying to judge just
how far he could go, Simon obviously decided to risk
it. 'You never did,' he gibed.

Although Jared maintained his easy stance, there
was an infinitesimal change in him—hard to know
what it was, but both she and Simon recognised it. A
slight shift of balance? A tightening of muscles? 'Too
far,' Jared warned, almost pleasantly.

Fascinated against her will by the rapport between
them, Lian silently cautioned Simon to back off.
Whether he felt it, or whether it was his own inner
judgement at work, Lian didn't know, but he suddenly gave best.

'Someone like Lian, then,' he qualified. And there was almost pleading in his dark eyes.

'For me or for you?' Jared asked gently. With a wry smile, he added rather sadly, 'You're learning too fast. Growing too fast—and I hope you will always remember that one of the most important things a man can learn is when to back off.' Eyeing his son with compassion, he reached out to ruffle his hair. 'I have some papers I need to go through; I'll be in the study if you want me.' Turning on his heel, he walked out.

Glancing at Simon, rather touched by his words, whether meant or not, Lian smiled at him. 'Thank you.'

With an embarrassed shrug, he got to his feet. 'I'm going upstairs to work on my computer.'

'All right.'

When he'd gone, she stared blindly at the television. She'd almost offered to split her duties. Almost. The impulsive gesture had hovered on the tip of her tongue, only to be swallowed. She didn't *want* to be a housekeeper. She wanted to sail *her* yacht, with *her* crew, in the round-the-world race due to start next month. And she couldn't. And she couldn't use Jared and his son as substitutes ... Was that what she was trying to do? How the hell did anyone ever know? And as the all too familiar despair washed over her she grabbed almost frantically at the paper in an effort to distract her thoughts.

When Jared returned half an hour later, she continued to pretend absorption in the paper. She was aware of him standing watching her, was prepared to ignore him. What she wasn't prepared for was him whisking the paper from her hands.

Folding it, he tossed it on to the table, then sat opposite her, hunched forward, arms along his thighs. 'This housekeeper business is getting out of hand. How long are you prepared to stay?' he asked bluntly.

'I don't know,' she confessed.

'He likes you...'

'I *know* that!' she exclaimed in exasperation. 'I like him too, but I don't *want* to be a housekeeper!'

'Then what *do* you want to do?'

'I don't know! But I can't keep drifting!' she exclaimed almost in despair. 'I have to take charge of my life.'

'Then let's look at it from another direction,' he insisted. 'See if we can't reach a compromise. How much do you know of what's been going on this past week?'

'Not very much, but I——'

'No, because I haven't told you,' he continued determinedly, 'because I've been shut in on myself. I'm sorry.' Pulling thoughtfully at his lower lip, his eyes unfocused as he stared at her, he began quietly, 'Briefly, then, I'm an engineer. Or was. Bridges, dams, whatever. It's what I like doing. What I was trained to do. My father owned an engineering works, inherited it from his father who had begun it, built it up from nothing. He expected that one day I would work there, eventually take over from him, follow in the family footsteps. I declined. It wasn't what I wanted. I wanted to travel, build monuments to myself, not to a grandfather I had never known, or a father I had never liked. Then, six months ago, he had a heart attack, and died, and he achieved in death what he couldn't in life.

'A lot of people worked for him. A lot of people feared for their jobs, their futures, and they looked upon me as a natural successor. Someone to solve their problems for them. I found I didn't have the necessary courage to refuse. So, reluctantly, I agreed to do what I could. When I began going through the books, invoices, orders, I found it was all in one hell of a mess. The management were incompetent, partly because of my father's arrogant refusal to drag the firm into the twentieth century, and partly from complacency—and you were right,' he admitted with a wry smile, 'I do expect people to jump when I say so. They didn't, so I put someone in to sort them all out. They'd lost big contracts, important customers, who, naturally enough, were beginning to look around for a more efficient firm—and that I *don't* like.

'The works bears my name, and, even though it wasn't through any fault of mine that it got into such a sorry state, it is still my name! So, as I said, I put an experienced man in, and thought in my innocence that I would only have to hold a watching brief while I got on with my own life, got Simon back on to an even keel after Nan died—do you know about Nan?'

'Only that she looked after him after your wife died.'

'Yes.' For a moment, Jared's face was soft, fond, as he remembered his wife? Or Nan?

'She looked after us both. And then some bastard drunk-driver ploughed into her, killed her instantly—and she seems irreplaceable.' Bringing himself back to the present with an effort, he continued, 'And then, a few weeks ago, I called in, looked at the books, and found things very little different, despite verbal assurances that orders were picking up. I uprooted poor

Simon, rented this cottage, dragged one of my secretaries down from my London office, and for the past two weeks have been, I hope successfully, persuading the bank to hold off from demanding the repayment of the loan my father stupidly took out; wooing back the big customers; updating the machinery—and generally making a nuisance of myself.

'I've caused hatred in some breasts, relief in others, and confusion to the rest. And when it's profitable I'm going to sell the damned thing! Lowe's Engineering can become someone else's problem. So, my dear Miss Grayson, there you have it in a nutshell. And if you could see your way clear to remaining here for perhaps another month you would have my most heartfelt and fervent gratitude.'

Staring at him, her face part exasperated, part thoughtful, Lian's mind picked up on stupid irrelevancies. One of his secretaries? How many did he have, for goodness' sake? And he spoke as though his London firm was enormous, but how could that be so if he was only an engineer?

'Well?' he barked.

'Oh, Jared, I don't know.'

'Two weeks, then,' he argued. 'How much difference can that possibly make?'

She had no idea, only that it seemed wise to get out of his orbit. Why? And, as he had so rightly said, what difference would two weeks make? 'And then you will go back to building your bridges?' she asked, knowing she was deliberately prevaricating. 'Go back where you came from?' Wherever that was.

'Yes, hopefully, and devote my time and energy to my son instead of a company that I never wanted, and could very well have done without. So? Yes?'

He made it very hard for her to refuse. Made her sound petty. With a big sigh, knowing she was probably being stupid, she gave a reluctant nod. 'But only two weeks!'

'Two weeks,' he agreed, and now that he had got his own way he smiled, rather smugly, she thought. Glancing at his watch, he added, 'My secretary will be here in a minute; I have some urgent letters I want to dicta——' Breaking off, he suddenly turned to look at the television that no one had bothered to turn off.

Following his gaze, Lian stared at the picture of herself on the screen, and froze.

' . . . will be sadly missing the delectable Lian Grayson,' the unknown announcer droned on, until now unheard, 'which only . . .'

Simon reappeared. 'Dad . . . Hey, that's Lian!'

'Ssh,' his father warned as he continued to stare at the television.

' . . . and certainly proves that planning and hard work are no guarantee that fate will leave you alone. She was to have been the first woman skipper of a mixed crew to take part in the round-the-world yacht race due to start in two weeks' time, and now both honour and challenge have been denied her. David Hanson has today been nominated as replacement, and although he will no doubt feel for Miss Grayson he can only be delighted by his own good fortune.'

David had been nominated? she thought incredulously. David? Well, how was that for rubbing salt into the wound? And as the picture of a laughing, wind-swept Lian was replaced by the obviously ecstatic, fair-haired man, the fair-haired man who had once professed to love her, she gave a bitter smile. Suddenly becoming aware that two pairs of identical dark eyes were staring at her in both accusation and astonishment, she got quickly to her feet and went out. Hurrying up to her room, she carefully closed the door behind her. Bastard, she thought, her vision blurred by tears. So he now had all he wanted. Not satisfied with taking her love, he had now taken her yacht, and her crew. Had her friends known he might be nominated? If so, no wonder they had seemed awkward.

Eyes closed, head back against the wood, Lian fought to retain her composure, fought to quell the bitterness. She had been doing so well, putting it behind her, and now it was all back, a stark reminder of all she had lost. It was so bloody unfair! She could eventually, she thought, have come to terms with losing her place, because it had after all been an accident. But to have David as the new skipper, triumphant, sneering . . .

The soft tap behind her made her jump. Moving away, she walked to stand at the window, her back to the room.

'Messing about in boats?' Jared exclaimed. 'Some messing! Oh, Lian, why in God's name didn't you say?'

'Why? What difference would it have made?' she asked emptily.

'None, to me, but one hell of a lot to you, I should imagine. You must have been heartbroken!'

'Yes.'

'And what on earth ever made you want to be a yacht skipper?' he asked in obvious astonishment as he moved up behind her, and gently turned her round. 'It seems to me the most extraordinary thing to want to be. For a man, yes . . .'

'Don't be——'

'Sexist?' he interrupted with a smile. 'I wasn't. I don't know much about yacht racing, but the little I've seen, or read about, it seems incredibly hard work, incredible determination for so little reward.'

'I didn't do it for the reward,' she denied. 'I did it for the challenge, for the sheer love of doing it. The companionship, the courage—the fun.'

'But to spend the better part of your life getting soaking wet...'

'Broken nails,' she murmured in the same empty, distant voice. 'Tacky hair...'

'Yes,' he agreed. 'And you're such a feminine-looking woman.'

'Most of us are. You think we should have arms like a wrestler? Thighs like a stevedore? Things have advanced a little since the days of the galley slave, you know.'

'I know. But I just find it so incomprehensible!'

'So I gathered,' she managed drily.

Tilting up her chin with one finger, he asked softly, 'And David Hanson? Who was he?'

Knocking his hand away, she abruptly turned back to the window.

'You're bitter because he got to be captain instead of you? Because they dropped you when you injured your back?'

'Leave it, Jared,' she said drearily, 'I don't want to talk about it.'

'It explains a lot,' he went on as though she hadn't spoken. 'I sometimes wondered at the sad light in your eyes...'

'And you didn't ask?' she demanded waspishly. 'My, my.'

'Ah, don't. And I do have some feelings, you know, some sensitivity.'

'Yes, I know, I'm sorry.'

'So who was David Hanson?'

'Oh, for goodness' sake! Some bastard who professed to love me in order to get introductions to important, influential people! Gain entry into a world that tends to be exclusive! All right?'

'And when he'd gained entry he dropped you?'

'Yes,' she agreed stiffly.

'And hurt you very badly,' he commented softly.

'Yes, he hurt me very badly, and made me angry, and disgusted with myself...'

'And very, very determined to beat him at his own game?' he guessed.

'Something like that. He dismissed me, and all women, I think, as not competitive enough, not strong enough for crewing round-the-world yachts.'

'And so you set out to prove him wrong.'

'And succeeded in proving him wrong,' she corrected, and then, as though the words had been dammed up inside her too long, she burst out, 'And for what? Two years of hard work, of finding a sponsor, training, working up the crew—and then some idiot tossed it all away.'

'How?'

'By falling on me, that's how! We were having a party on board the yacht, celebrating getting another sponsor, someone lost their balance, fell against me—and I landed awkwardly on some tackle. A stupid, *stupid* accident. Years of scrimping and saving, of doing odd jobs to pay my mortgage, eat. Every spare minute sailing, practising—wiped away in seconds. All my dreams gone.'

'And not enough time left to regain your fitness.'

'I'll never regain my fitness, not enough for that, anyway. And what sponsor is going to take a chance on damaged goods?' Lian tried very hard to mask her bitterness, but she didn't think she succeeded very well. 'I thought I'd be better away from the sea,' she continued almost reflectively, 'but I'm not. I miss it. Damnably.'

'Yes,' he agreed sympathetically, 'because even if you can't sail it as you want to you need to see it, hear it.'

'Yes. So, when I've finished here, I'll sell my flat and go down to stay with my father in Devon.'

'You didn't want to stay with him after the accident?'

'No. He was too sympathetic, too kind. He made me worse. Self-pitying. I *hate* self-pity!' she said savagely.

'So you picked yourself up, dusted yourself off, and tried to start all over again. As a chauffeur.'

'Yes.'

'Because you could,' Jared murmured, repeating the words she had used that day in the kitchen. 'I'm sorry,' he said gently. 'Life can be a real bitch sometimes, can't it?'

'Yes.'

'And what about all your friends? Your crew? They don't keep in touch? Or did you cut yourself off?'

Very astute, Jared, she thought. 'Yes,' she admitted. 'I found I couldn't bear to see the sympathy in their eyes, feel their awkwardness.'

'So tonight was the first time that you knew David Hanson had been made skipper?'

'Yes. And I hope he bloody loses!' she said vengefully.

With a grunt of laughter, he patted her shoulder in a comforting gesture. 'That's the spirit; hate the bastard.'

'Yes, not much else I can do, is there?'

'Sabotage?' he offered helpfully. 'And there's always next time to look forward to. Beat him next time, Lian.'

'Perhaps.' But she knew there would never be a next time. Her back would never be strong enough again for yacht racing. Oh, she'd still be able to sail, potter about on the water, but not do what she had trained to do, fought to do, compete in a man's world...

'It was quite an accolade, though, wasn't it? Woman skipper of a mixed crew.'

'Yes,' she agreed with empty pride. 'It was quite an achievement. But without the proof of winning, the proof of doing well, it doesn't mean very much, does it?'

'Of course it does. It means they had faith that you could. Confidence in your ability, and that's a hell of a lot more than some people ever have.'

'I suppose,' she sighed. 'And that sounds like the doorbell,' she added as she heard a distant ring.

Cocking his head in a listening attitude, Jared nodded. 'That will be Heather. My secretary. You'll be all right now?'

'Yes, of course. Do you want me to make some tea, or something?'

'No, that's OK, I'll do it.'

'Dad?' Simon yelled up the stairs. 'Heather's here!'

'Coming!' he shouted. Giving her a faint, compassionate smile, he went out and she heard him run lightly down the stairs.

She remained where she was for a moment, just standing, staring at nothing, remembering the day that her dreams had been smashed. And it was futile. Destructive and futile. 'The Moving Finger writes; and, having writ, Moves on...' Yeah. So come on, Lian, snap out of it; who the hell cares about David bloody Hanson? One door shuts and another opens... Platitudes, but what else was there? Glancing at her watch, seeing with surprise that it was after six, and belatedly realising that none of them had had anything to eat, she found she had a sudden yearning for pancakes. Pancakes? Well, why not? If you could have turkey for Easter, why not pancakes in July? With a rather poor imitation of her old mischievous smile, she straightened her shoulders in determination and opened the door. As he'd said, life could be a bitch.

Simon was hunched on the top of the stairs. Christopher Robin without Bear. Someone else with a crumpled world. Walking quietly along the landing, she hunkered down to join him. 'I don't know why it is,' she ventured quietly, 'but stairs always seem to be the best place for thinking. And you look very thoughtful indeed.'

Giving her a quick smile that lacked his usual impish charm, he pronounced slowly, 'Dad said I wasn't to ask you...'

'But it proved too hard to resist?' she teased.

Looking relieved, he grinned. 'Were you famous?' he exclaimed endearingly.

'Heavens, no. Infamous, maybe.'

'Is that the opposite of famous?'

'Yes. Sorry, I didn't mean to be flip.'

'That's all right. Dad does it all the time. Lian?' he asked hesitantly. 'Is it hard to talk about?'

Surprised by his astuteness, she nodded. 'Yes. It sort of sits inside me, hurting. Like a big lump that won't go away.'

'And you want people to know, without you having to say, don't you?'

'Yes,' she agreed gently. 'Like you when Nan died?' she guessed.

'Yes.'

'Do you want to talk about her now? She was special, wasn't she?'

'Yes. She was nice. Funny and nice,' he added, his face sad for a moment. 'She winked a lot, and had a big apron that smelled of cakes.' And then he gave a wide smile as the memories of her began to tumble back. 'She said I was better than sliced bread, because my middle wasn't doughy. She meant——'

'That you were brave and tough and didn't go to pieces when the crust fell off.'

'Yes!' he laughed. 'Oh, yes.'

'And I was lucky, wasn't I? Because I didn't die. Just got a bit hurt, and couldn't do what I really wanted to do, and so I took it out on everyone else. But it surely did knock me for six,' she sighed. 'I was angry, and miserable, and cross with myself for being that way, but I couldn't seem to help it. So I'm sorry if I haven't seemed to understand your own problems.'

Looking surprised, Simon denied, 'Yes, you have! You don't fuss over me. You don't call me a sweet little boy; or a poor little boy; or tell me to run away and play! Yuk!'

Who, she wondered, had had the temerity to tell him to run away and play? A smile in her eyes, she found she wanted to hug him. He was such a delightful mixture of wise and woeful. Adult and child. 'Fancy some pancakes?'

Staring at her in astonishment, he suddenly gave a slow, wide smile. 'Yeah!' Leaping to his feet, he was halfway down the stairs before she'd even got up.

With a rueful little smile, she followed him. What a pity all the world's troubles couldn't be cured by something as simple as pancakes.

Finding all the necessary ingredients in the well-stocked kitchen, thanks to Mary, she presumed, she also found two small frying-pans, and, wielding one each, they made pancakes. Tossed pancakes, and both, for a glorious half-hour, descended to nursery level. They were sitting side by side, eating the fruits of their labour, both with sugar round their mouths, when Jared walked in, closely followed by his secretary. He halted on the threshold as though he couldn't believe his eyes.

Staring from their laughing faces to their empty plates, he demanded, 'Where's mine?'

'In the mixing-bowl,' Simon told him with a wide, sugary grin.

'Thanks a bunch!' he retorted, a smile in his eyes for them both. Turning to his secretary, he asked teasingly, 'Want some pancakes?'

'Heavens, no!' she denied. 'I haven't eaten them since I was a child.'

'Haven't you?' Jared demanded in astonishment; quite foiling her desire, either deliberately, or inadvertently, to make the other two look foolish, he commiserated, 'Poor you. You've met Lian of course,' he added, quickly changing the subject.

'Yes. Hello, Lian,' she greeted with a superior and rather condescending little smile.

'Heather.' And perhaps because she was still feeling a little raw, and because she really didn't like the other girl, and perhaps, more honestly, because she didn't know how Jared felt about her, Lian was tempted into behaving rather badly. On one level she could understand Heather's dislike at finding another woman in her beloved Jared's orbit, but there was no earthly need to be patronising just because she thought Lian merely the chauffeur and therefore beneath notice. Jared, quite rightly, didn't make distinctions, something that Heather was probably well aware of, and added even more fuel to her dislike of Lian.

'Are you sure you wouldn't like some pancakes?' she queried mischievously, knowing full well that Heather was torn between a desire to agree with her adored Jared, and sticking to her own guns. 'There's plenty of mixture left.'

'No, thank you. Perhaps a cup of tea before I get on with my work?'

'Certainly,' she agreed equably. Turning to the man silently watching them, and with deliberate, and rather naughty provocation, she asked, 'Jared? Would you like yours now? Or later?'

A faint twitch to his lips, he asked softly, 'Will the mixture keep?'

A *double entendre*? Yes, of course it was! Her eyes sparkling with delight at finding someone willing to play, she gave a slow, slightly wicked smile. And even if she was wrong, and it was a case of mixture being what he said and what he meant, where was the harm in being ambiguous? A little ambiguity would add spice. Wouldn't it? And spice had been sadly missing from her life of late. 'Oh, yes,' she agreed, her voice deliberately husky, 'and mixture is often better left to stand. Don't you think?'

'Oh, indubitably,' he drawled, his own eyes full of appreciative amusement. 'So, pancakes later? Tea for now? For two? In the study?'

'Certainly.'

When they had both gone out, she and Simon gave in to a fit of the giggles. Not that Simon would have understood the undercurrents between herself and his father. At least she hoped he didn't—and that she had. If, of course, undercurrents there had been. Heather hadn't been too sure either, and that pleased her enormously. You've got a nasty nature, Lian, she told herself. Yes. And why? Because you want Jared for yourself? Rubbish! She liked him, she freely admitted that, but it was nothing more. He was manipulative, like David ... No, he wasn't, but it might be safer to go on thinking so. Anyway, it wasn't serious, just a little light flirtation. Where was the harm in that?

It was gone ten before she heard the front door close behind Heather, and Jared's slow footsteps echo along the hall. And she was nervous. How silly. Nervous of what, for goodness' sake? Pancakes? The thought made her smile. She was still smiling when Jared walked into the lounge and halted in front of her.

'Pancakes?' he asked softly, and she gave him a deliberately provocative grin.

'Of course. How do you like them?'

'Oh, soft, pliant, with just a hint of firmness. Nicely—rounded.' His eyes were full of laughter, his cheeks creased with the effort of suppressing his own

smile, and she felt a lick of excitement along her
nerves.

'Are you flirting with me?' she managed to ask
more or less evenly.

'Reciprocating,' he corrected softly. Holding out
his hand, he waited until she'd put her own into it,
before pulling her gently to her feet. 'You have a
lovely, deliciously wicked smile,' he told her in the
same soft voice.

'Thank you,' she whispered, her eyes still locked
with his. 'And so, my friend, do you.' She needed to
swallow, she found, needed to consciously regulate
her breathing, which seemed determined to get out of
control. She hadn't meant this to happen—or had she?
He was still loosely holding her hand, yet he seemed
closer, and she had no idea whether she had moved,
or he had. Lowering her eyes to his mouth, she admired its shape, its texture, its—nearness.

As though she were drugged, as though their actions had already been programmed, they leaned ever
nearer to each other until their mouths just brushed,
just tingled with the contact before a newer, warmer
emotion took its place. No pressure, no hint of
passion, just a gentle exploration, and Lian closed
her eyes the better to savour it. Touch and part; touch
and part; taste, explore, a little sigh, a warm puff of
breath. Warm, strong palms ascending; elbows, upper
arms, shoulders; fingers just touching her neck; a delicious shiver of awareness; a zone found for, hopefully, future reference.

Barely aware of what she was doing, she gave a
little sighing sound of pleasure, slid her palms up his
strong chest, briefly felt the slightly accelerated
heartbeat before moving on to link her fingers behind

his neck and give her body room to rest comfortably against his. To feel his warmth against her. Thigh to thigh, breast to breast...

'Dad? Oh.'

'Go away,' Jared said thickly, 'I'm busy.'

'Oh. Right.'

Lian heard the door close, the scamper of footsteps, but found it took too much effort to lift her lids, to straighten. She felt enfolded in warmth, in comfort, in pleasure, and all her blood, energy seemed to have drained downwards. Gravity was a wonderful thing, she thought hazily as she continued to explore the pleasure of his mouth, allowed him to explore hers. His strong fingers were in her thick hair as he held her head cradled, found another zone, which had the added advantage of making her arch her body towards him, her head back, and, given the easier access, his lips teased hers apart, played with them in a warm, intimate game that delighted and aroused her. It aroused him, too.

Without disturbing him, distracting his concentration, she lowered her arms, slid them round his waist, tugged his shirt free, found the warm flesh of his back—a tactile pleasure, a delight after so many months of denial. David had left her with no taste for dalliance, and that made her doubly the fool, because she was a warm-blooded creature who needed affection, loving, the warmth of human contact.

'This is so nice,' she breathed when his mouth briefly left hers to explore her earlobe.

'Mm, *vive le* Shrove Tuesday,' he mumbled back, and she gave a hiccuping little snort of laughter. Lifting his head, his eyes smiled down into hers. 'Welcome back to the human race.'

'Thank you.'

'Welcome. I have to go and tuck Simon in—and I hate to be mundane but oh, Lian, I'm starving!'

'Pancakes?'

'Please.'

'Lemon and sugar?'

'Naturally, what other way is there?' Dropping a brief kiss on her nose, he pushed his shirt back in, gave a funny little sigh, and went up to say goodnight to his son.

A pleasant glow inside her, she went to get his meal ready. An interlude that was as unexpected as it was delightful. She felt no embarrassment, or awkwardness; it was just something nice that had happened. Quite convinced that her emotions were entirely under her control, she gave him a warm smile when he walked into the kitchen—and the doorbell rang.

CHAPTER THREE

'I'LL go, you eat your pancakes.' Indicating for Jared to sit, Lian put the plate before him, and went out to answer the door.

Heather stood there, and Lian stared at her in surprise. 'Hello, forget something?'

'No,' she denied, with an aloof little toss of her head, and then her eyes narrowed on Lian's tumbled hair and warmly flushed face, and drew the obvious conclusion. 'I need to see Jared. Excuse me.' Without waiting for Lian to move, she pushed past her rudely.

She hadn't looked hurt, Lian decided as she closed the front door, a thoughtful frown in her eyes, only angry. If she had looked upset, Lian would have been sorry, regretful, because she wouldn't deliberately cause anyone pain, no matter how rude they were being; but she hadn't, which meant what? That she wasn't in love with Jared, only wanted him? Because he was attractive and, presumably, wealthy? Because she had come to think of him as her property? Turning to face the other girl, Lian searched her angry face. 'He's having something to eat. In the kitchen,' she added to herself as Heather walked rapidly along the hall and into the kitchen, where her frosty manner rapidly underwent a transformation.

No, not in love with him, Lian decided as she followed the other girl, then gave a faint smile at the helpless female act she was putting on. Glancing at Jared, she could detect no trace of affection, just the pleasant behaviour of a man towards his secretary. Much the way he treated herself, in fact ...

'So stupid,' Heather was deriding herself, 'but the silly thing just died on me.'

'Out of petrol?' Jared asked helpfully. 'Or it could be a flat battery.'

'No, no, I'm sure not, and I am so sorry to interrupt your meal,' Heather continued, still determinedly ignoring Lian, 'but would you be so kind as to run me back to my hotel?'

'Sure ...' he began.

'I can do it,' Lian offered, and knew that it wasn't prompted by kindness. That was the second time she'd been a bit bitchy, and she was beginning to be disturbed by this new and not very likeable trait that was coming out in her character. However, having offered ... 'Come on, I'll run you back while Jared finishes his pancakes.' Deliberately avoiding his eyes, she called, 'I won't be long.' With a very chagrined Heather following her, she picked up the car keys, and made her way out to the car.

'You'll have to direct me,' she said quietly.

'It's the other side of town,' Heather informed her coldly.

And did you really expect anything else, like thanks? Lian asked herself as she unlocked the doors. Walking round to the driver's side, she got behind the wheel.

'Very sure of yourself, aren't you, Miss Grayson?' Heather retorted. 'And if you think I missed that little by-play earlier I didn't! But perhaps I should warn you that it doesn't mean anything. He flirts with everyone.'

'Does he?'

'Yes! He's a very masculine man, and he likes women.'

'Including yourself, I take you to mean,' she said softly as she fired the engine.

'Yes. Not that he has any need to flirt with me, because our relationship is very secure.'

Someone else being ambiguous? Lian wondered. 'And you don't mind him flirting with other women?' she asked disbelievingly.

'Of course not; it doesn't mean anything, I told you.'

'I'd mind,' Lian murmured before she could stop herself, 'if he were mine.'

'Which he isn't!'

'No.'

'And,' Heather added, presumably for good measure, 'we understand each other very well! I wouldn't like to see you get hurt,' she added magnanimously.

Liar; she looked as though she'd like nothing better.

'I realise of course that he needs you at the moment to look after poor little Simon, and to drive him around, but...'

'Simon isn't poor,' Lian pointed out, beginning to get really quite angry by this very silly girl.

'I did not mean literally——'

'I know you didn't.'

'Will you kindly stop interrupting?' she snapped.

With an involuntary little smile, because the words were so reminiscent of her own to Jared that first day, Lian hastily straightened her face when Heather continued.

'There is also,' she gritted, presumably in the face of what she thought was Lian's refusal to take her seriously, 'a little proverb, which perhaps you should remember.'

'Many a slip 'twixt the cup and the lip?' Lian offered, quite unable to help herself. 'Many hands make light work? He who laughs last, et cetera?'

'No. He who pays the piper, calls the tune. And this particular tune is nearly at an end. Or weren't you aware of that?' she asked sweetly. 'I'm afraid, Miss Grayson, that your employment is about to be terminated.'

'Yes,' she agreed more sombrely. How foolish to have forgotten that, in which case it was really rather stupid, and pointless, to get into an argument with Heather. And yet surely his kiss had meant something? You don't go around kissing other women if you're already involved. Don't you? she asked herself cynically. David had. David had used anyone who would advance his cause. And, although half of what Heather said could probably be discounted as the opinions of a jealous woman, she did know Jared a great deal better than herself. And she should, had she been a nice, charitable, sort of person, have pitied Heather, because if Jared really was like David, using people for his own ends, then she and Heather had a great deal in common. And wouldn't she, if she had found out that David was using other women when she thought he still loved her, have been just as waspish? Yes, she would. In which case...

Halting outside the hotel, she turned impulsively to the other girl. 'Look, I'm sorry we got off to a bad start; I think...'

With a hard, derisory stare, Heather got out without even waiting for Lian to finish.

And there endeth the first lesson, she told herself. Never try to befriend a woman who thinks she's been scorned. With a long sigh, she returned to the house.

Jared was still sitting in the kitchen where she had left him, and she stared at him for a moment, trying, she supposed, to see past his public face. See the inner man.

'Everything all right?' he asked with a little lift of one eyebrow.

'Yes, fine,' she agreed hastily.

'And is Heather arranging for her car to be collected? Or does she wish me to?'

'Oh,' she murmured lamely, 'I forgot to ask. Do you want me to ring her?'

'No, Lian,' he denied with wry humour. 'I think I'd better.'

'Mm.' With a sheepish little nod, she walked across to feel the teapot. 'Tea?'

'Already made,' he informed her drily.

Pouring herself a cup, she sat opposite him. How do you ask a man if his kisses meant anything? she wondered. How do——?

'Don't try to be too clever, will you?' he asked softly.

'I'm sorry?'

'So you should be,' he approved, deliberately misunderstanding, 'and I would be enormously grateful if you would refrain from upsetting my secretary. She accompanied me down here as a favour, because the secretary at the engineering works was quite useless. She's making do in a local hotel, has to put herself out considerably for my benefit, and I will not have her upset. All right?'

'Yes,' she said quietly. Message received and understood. If it came to a contest, Heather would win hands down.

'Good. Because if I have to expend time and energy smoothing down her ruffled feathers, I shall not be best pleased.'

'I only offered to run her home,' she reproved, but found that she couldn't quite meet his eyes.

'Yes, and we both know why. Leave her alone, Lian, she's not in your league.'

'You don't know what my league is,' she muttered. 'And that sounded suspiciously like an insult.'

'It wasn't meant to be; I was merely trying to point out that you're a great deal older than her, and presumably more experienced ... At least I hope you are,' he tacked on softly.

'Meaning?'

'Meaning I wouldn't want you to read anything more into our earlier behaviour than was meant. It was something nice, and pleasant, and uncomplicated. And that's the way I would like it to stay.'

She might sometimes have been a fool in the past, but she wasn't stupid, neither was she lacking in pride, and, whatever her own private thoughts about his kiss had been, Lian was damned if Jared would ever know of them now. 'That's how I would like it to stay too,' she admitted, almost convinced that it was the truth. 'And I am not a *great* deal older than her,' she added pointedly.

'No,' he agreed with a bland smile, 'not a *great* deal. Not in years, anyway. However, that isn't what I wanted to talk to you about. The summer holidays start next week, and——'

'And the thought of leaving Simon to run riot while you finalise your business plans,' she finished for him, 'doesn't bear thinking about.' And if he wanted to think of her as hard and experienced, then let him, because it looked as though she had been right about him, and he was like David. She should have understood that his behaviour when they first met was the real Jared, and that the charming and likeable man he had since become had been acting, a calculated ploy to make her stay; and that disappointed her very much.

'No, it doesn't,' he agreed. 'He will need constant supervision, and, seeing as I shan't require a chauffeur for much longer, but will probably need the car tomorrow, I will arrange for the hire of a little runabout for you to use. Maybe you could take him out for trips or something.'

'Of course, although it hardly seems worth the expense for the short time I'll be here.'

'My son is always worth the expense,' he reproved almost absently. His head on one side, he observed her quietly for a moment. 'What's wrong?'

'Wrong? Why should anything be wrong?'

'I don't know, that's why I'm asking. You're suddenly wearing your frosty face. Because I teased you about being older than Heather?'

'No.'

'Then what? Because you are angry about something, aren't you?'

'No.' But she was; she was angry about his assumption that she might read more into his kiss than was meant. Angry that she had, and angry that he even felt the need to point it out. And angry and disappointed that he wasn't the man she had thought him.

Still watching her, he persisted, 'Is it because of the sailing? The nearness of the race? There'll be a lot more media coverage, I imagine. A continual raking up of the past, explanations about the change of skipper.'

'Yes, there will.' Better for him to think that than that she had almost made a fool of herself over him. Wrenching her mind back to the reason for her being here at all, she added sombrely, 'It starts next week.'

'I'm sorry,' he said gently. 'Inadequate, I know——' Breaking off, he lurched forward in his seat as a loud yell rent the air.

'Oh, hell, now what?' Scraping back his chair, he shot upright.

'That yell came from outside...' Shoving her own chair back, her own troubles forgotten, Lian hurriedly followed Jared as he wrenched open the kitchen door. Skidding out into the yard, they both stared upwards in astonishment. Simon was stretched between his bedroom window and the branch of the tree. His young face looked, for once, very frightened.

'Oh, my God——' Jared began.

'I can't get back!' Simon shouted. 'My foot's stuck!'

'You catch him, I'll unstick his foot,' Lian offered hastily. Hurrying inside and upstairs, she raced into Simon's room. The hem of his pyjama trousers was firmly caught on the window-catch, she saw, and, shaking her head in rather amused despair at the things children got up to, she hurried across to him. Taking a secure grip on his ankles, she peered downward to where Jared waited, then looked to see how firm a grip Simon had on the tree.

'Are you holding on tight?' she asked him, and when he gave a muffled affirmative she gently released the caught material. Holding his feet steady, she said, 'All right, can you swing yourself across? Oh, yes, you can,' she answered herself as the boy agilely swung free. Jared caught his legs in a firm grip, and Simon let go.

'What the hell were you doing?' she heard Jared demand, but his son's reply was indistinct as his father urged him inside.

Walking back down and pushing once more into the kitchen, she stared at a very chastened-looking Simon. 'Playing Tarzan, were we?' she asked.

'Don't bloody encourage him!' Jared retorted. 'He could have broken his neck!'

'But didn't,' Lian soothed. With the automatic urge to soothe, she decided that it might be wise to separate these two before Jared could go way over the top, and Simon could resent it, which, judging by the mutinous expression on his face, he was about to. She held out her hand. 'Come on, back to bed, you have school tomorrow.' The alacrity with which he obeyed was comical.

'I was only trying to see if I'd grown enough to do it,' he told her with sulky indignation. 'He didn't need to carry on as though I'd done it just to annoy him. And he was the one who told me how he used to climb out of his bedroom window when he was a boy!' he added even more indignantly.

Hiding her smile, Lian steered him into the bathroom to wash his filthy hands. 'He was frightened,' she explained quietly. 'He loves you a great deal, you know, and when you only have one chick, well, unfairly perhaps, all your hopes and dreams are centred on that one person, which makes it a bit of a responsibility. And you're not exactly un-adventurous, are you?' she teased. 'There are only so many frights one man can withstand. And at the rate you're going he'll be grey before the year is out.'

'He still didn't need to shout at me like that! I said I was sorry!'

'So will he be when the fright's worn off,' she promised. 'Come on, into bed with you.' Holding the duvet invitingly open, she then tucked it round him when he dived inside. Perching on the edge of the bed, she smiled at the boy's woebegone face. 'I expect you gave yourself a bit of fright as well, didn't you?'

'Yeah.' With a sudden enchanting grin, Simon turned over and snuggled down. ' 'Night, Lian.'

'Goodnight.' Walking across, she re-latched the window and drew the curtains across. Light evenings were obviously too much of a temptation to an ad-venturous boy. And why she was championing Jared's cause, she didn't know!

Yes, she did, of course she did; driving a wedge between father and son would be a despicable thing to do, and in all fairness Jared hadn't asked her to fall in—become fond, she mentally substituted, be-cause she wasn't falling in love with him. The very notion was quite absurd.

Reluctantly returning to the kitchen, she took in Jared's tight expression, and sighed. 'About to tell me to mind my own business?' she guessed, correctly, as it happened. 'I'll apologise if you want me to,' she offered with a slight stiffness that she seemed unable to dispel, 'but I thought it was a case of least said, soonest mended.'

His obvious internal struggle was brief. 'Yes,' he agreed heavily. 'You're probably right.'

'Mm. Galling, ain't it?'

His look said it all, and then he gave a grunt of laughter. 'I think, Miss Grayson, that I would have found it intolerable to be one of your crew.'

Would you? she wondered. Yes, perhaps he would. She didn't think he would take orders easily, and especially not from a woman. Forcing herself to be pleasant, when all she wanted was to go up to her room and have a good think, get her mind and emotions back on an even keel, she murmured, 'Whatever, but you can't in all fairness crib just because your son tries to do the very thing you once told him you did. Can you?'

'No.' Getting to his feet, Jared eyed her silently for some minutes. 'You . . .' he began, then, with a little shake of his head, he said quietly, 'I have one or two things to clear up in the study; I'll see you in the morning. Goodnight, Lian.'

' 'Night.'

Rinsing the cups and his dirty plate, she left them to drain before going up to her room. It took her ages to get off to sleep, mostly because her mind would persist in going over everything Jared had ever said or done since she had first arrived. And all so damned pointless. Finally, determinedly, persuading herself that her feelings for him had only been generated because she'd been vulnerable, and that now that she knew the cause she would be in a much better position to deal with them, she forced herself to relax— only to have her mind go over it all again. She finally fell into a deep sleep in the early hours of the morning, which meant that she overslept. So did Jared, but she doubted that his failure to get up early had anything to do with a sleepless night. He'd probably been working late in the study.

'Didn't you hear the alarm?' he demanded grumpily before yelling for his son to get up.

Not bothering to answer, she shoved the kettle on the stove and hastily got out cornflakes and milk. There was then a mad scramble to get Simon ready for school, Lian ready to drive Jared to work, and for Jared to hunt fruitlessly for his briefcase, which improved nobody's temper.

'Have you seen it?' he demanded irritably.

'No I haven't— Simon, keep still!' she commanded as she tried to get his tie straight. 'Right. Dinner-money?'

'Yes, in my pocket—look, I have to go! I'll be late!'

'All right, go! I'll see you later.'

When Simon had grabbed his satchel and left, she began to stack the dirty dishes in the dishwasher hurriedly while Jared rang Heather to ask about his briefcase.

'She says she thought she gave it to you!' he accused as he strode back to the kitchen.

'Not to my knowledge, she didn't,' Lian frowned. 'When did she give it to me?'

'Last night—well, I don't have time to go into it now; there's a duplicate file in the office.' Glancing irritably at his watch, he grabbed the car keys. 'I'll drive myself...'

'You can't,' she denied. 'The car's booked in for a service.'

'Oh, damn. Well, come on, then!' he retorted impatiently. 'I haven't got all day to waste!' Thrusting the keys back at her, he pushed back into the hall. 'And make sure it's damned well ready in time for you to pick me up.'

Grabbing her bag, feeling muddled and only half ready, Lian hastened after him. When she climbed into the driver's seat, she heard his exclamation from the back seat.

'What?' she asked, twisting round to see.

'My briefcase,' he said harshly. 'Thanks a lot, Lian; leaving it in the car was a really good idea!'

'I didn't!' she denied as she fitted the key into the ignition.

'Well, somebody did!'

You? she asked him silently. With an irritated shake of her head, she drove quickly along the lane to the main road. Dropping him off at his office, he muttered indistinctly as he climbed from the car, 'I'll ring when I'm ready to leave.'

With a little nod, she waited until he'd thrust through the plate-glass doors of the building before driving the car to the garage. With the strictest of instructions to the mechanic to have it ready and delivered back at the house by lunchtime, she took a cab home. She felt exhausted.

She spent the rest of the day pottering about, tidying up, having a coffee with Mary when she came in to sort something out for the evening meal. She did a test drive in the car when it was returned, leaving Mary to man the phone, signed for it, and then went up to shower and change and wait for the phone call from Jared. The telephone remained infuriatingly silent. She couldn't even ring her father, or any of her friends, for a chat, because, Murphy's Law being what it was, the very minute she was chatting to someone else would be the very minute that Jared would try to ring her.

At three, Mary popped back in, and, with a smile, explained, 'Heather just rang; apparently she couldn't get any reply from here. Jared wants picking up at four. All right?'

'Yes, fine. I wonder why she couldn't get any answer from here?' Lian frowned. 'I haven't been anywhere.' Walking across to the phone, she picked it up and listened for a dialling tone. 'Seems to be all right. Oh, well, thanks, Mary.'

'No problem. Want me to keep an eye on Simon? He'll be home before you get back, I expect.'

Still puzzled about the phone, Lian absently thanked her. Better ring the engineer to check the line, otherwise she knew who would get the blame for a non-functioning instrument.

Leaving herself plenty of time to get to the office, in case the traffic was bad, she'd barely drawn up outside the building when Jared came striding out. 'Where the hell have you been?' he demanded. 'It's four o'clock!'

'I know...'

'Well, don't apologise, will you?' he retorted sarcastically. 'And when I specifically designate a time I would be enormously grateful if you'd stick to it!'

'I did!'

'You did not! Three-thirty, I said! And I would have expected you to have enough sense to allow for traffic! You know damned well it's Simon's open evening, and now I'm going to be hellishly late!'

She hadn't known anything of the sort, but, knowing the futility of saying so in the mood he was in, she kept quiet about it. There didn't seem much point in explaining about the phone call either. Mary had obviously misunderstood what Heather had said, but where was the point in getting her into trouble as well? 'You wish to go straight to the school?' she asked in as neutral a voice as she could manage.

'Yes, Miss Grayson, I wish to go straight to the school.'

They were, of course, late. Simon had got fed up with waiting and had gone home. His teacher was irritated at having to wait around and was foolish enough to tell Jared so, which meant that by the time he returned to the car and pithily informed Lian of what she had put him through his temper was almost out of control. Then, to make bad worse, when they did get home Simon was nowhere to be found. Which was her fault, naturally.

By the time she got to bed that evening, she felt mangled; was hating Jared, and his son, and anyone daft enough to ever want to be a housekeeper. So why don't you leave? she asked herself. Because she'd given her word, because it wouldn't be fair to Simon, because... Oh, yeah? At least be honest with yourself. You won't leave, because you don't want to!

The morning brought no great improvement. Although it was a Saturday, Jared still had a mountain of work to get through.

'Heather will be coming over,' he told her flatly. 'Do you think you might manage some lunch for us?'

'Certainly,' she agreed stonily. 'Sandwiches?'

'Sandwiches will be fine.' Turning his glare on his son, who was busily pulling faces, he demanded, 'What the hell do you think you're doing?'

'Nothing,' Simon denied with an innocence that only a nine-year-old boy seemed able to achieve. 'Can I get down?'

'Yes. And stay out of trouble.'

'Sure. Peter's coming over; we'll only be in the barn.'

'It's the "only" that worries me. Go on, hop it.'

Scrambling down, he hurried out.

Avoiding Lian's glance, which she preferred to assume was because he was embarrassed by his behaviour the day before, and not because he was thoroughly disliking her, Jared disappeared into his study. Five minutes later, she heard Heather arrive. Obviously she'd got her car to start.

With nothing very much to do, because the cleaning woman had been in the day before, Lian tidied the kitchen, whisked the duster round the lounge, and then decided to go exploring. Jared, or Heather, could make their own damned coffee if they wanted it.

The woods and stream behind the house were her first target, and she halted to stare at the rope that dangled from a stout oak. Simon's work? So that he could swing himself across the water? Probably, and no doubt explained his wet state on the day of her arrival.

Transferring her gaze to the tree-tops that moved gently in the breeze, she sighed. A good sailing day. They'd be out now... Oh, shut up!

Turning determinedly away, she began to follow the stream, and was astonished to discover that it widened out into a large pool, fed by, at this time of year, a sluggishly running river. Picking up a handful of stones, she moodily dropped them one by one into the water. It looked, and sounded deep. It also smelled ever so slightly stagnant. Wrinkling her nose distastefully, she continued her walk.

She met a woman with a dog, a man with a spade, and as she walked towards the village she speculated on the need for one. Turf-cutting? Body-burying? Or for innocent use on an allotment somewhere? Disgusted with herself, mostly about making excuses for her need to stay, and feeling, for the first time she could remember, aimless, Lian bought herself an ice-cream in the village shop and began the slow walk home. She wasn't used to being idle, didn't quite know how to use up time. Read the books she had always meant to read? Take up knitting? No, Lian, what you have to do is leave, before you become even more involved with this family. And never see him again?

Dear Lord, Lian, but you're turning into an indecisive moron. What happened to all the get up and go? The fun? The laughter? Leave, that would be best. Go back to Devon, stay with Dad for a bit, learn to live with your limitations. With another long sigh, she pushed into the kitchen. Jared was standing at the sink, pouring boiling water into two mugs. He looked distant, and as moody as she felt. Trying to be objective, she stared at his closed face, his rumpled hair, his strong, hard body, his sensuous mouth... It really would be best to leave.

Still without looking at her, he removed the spoon he had been using to stir the coffee, and only when he had laid it carefully on the work-top did he turn. His eyes, for some odd reason, seemed darker. 'I knew that you and Heather were as different as two people can be,' he said quietly. 'Knew that you didn't particularly like her, but I did not think you would be unkind.'

'Unkind?' she queried blankly.

'Yes. Perhaps you expected she wouldn't tell me. But I've known Heather for two years. I know her moods, I know when she's happy, and I know when she's upset. Yesterday, I was too busy to query it, but this morning, when I found she was still upset, I asked her why. To her credit, she didn't want to tell me.'

Staring at him in astonishment, Lian asked blankly, 'Tell you what?'

'That you had been rude to her.'

'When?' she demanded.

'When you ran her back to her hotel.'

'Rubbish,' she retorted dismissively. 'I even tried to apologise...'

'For what?' he asked silkily. 'If you weren't rude, why the need to apologise?'

Narrowing her eyes on his face, a warning glitter in their depths, she leaned back against the doorframe, and folded her arms across her chest. 'I apologised,' she explained quietly, 'because I thought perhaps we had got off on the wrong foot, and obviously, very stupidly, imagined that we might start again, as friends.'

Leaning his hips against the work surface, and folding his own arms, he returned her stare. 'That's not my understanding of what happened.'

'No, so it would seem. So what did she say? Come on,' she encouraged with a tight little smile. 'Let's have it all, chapter and verse.'

'Well, unless you're an idiot, which you by no means are, you must know damned well what you said!' he retorted impatiently.

'I do. I'm merely interested to know what Heather said I said.'

'Which implies you think she lied to me.'

'Not necessarily; it might only be a question of interpretation.' And pigs might fly. 'So what did she say?'

'That you accused her of deliberately trying to promote my interest in her—romantically,' he said scathingly. 'She was very embarrassed.'

'Oh, I'll bet she was.'

'That you resented my closeness with her,' he continued through his teeth, 'and warned her off. You also told her that you thought Simon a poor little thing and needed looking after. True?'

'No. Not true. I really misjudged her, didn't I?' she retorted angrily.

'Meaning?'

'Meaning I'm obviously not as clever as I thought I was.'

'Obviously not,' he said tightly. 'So now perhaps you will tell me why?'

'Oh, no, Jared, I have absolutely no intention of telling you anything. You've made up your mind as to my guilt—understandable, I suppose, since you do, after all, know her a great deal better than you do me. Or think you do. But, unlike your little secretary, I have no intention of trying to justify myself, or tell tales out of school.'

'Well, you just admitted you were rude to her!' he snapped frustratedly.

'On the contrary, I admitted that I apologised for perhaps misunderstanding her. And that has to be the understatement of the year!'

'Which is no bloody answer at all! However, for the sake of peace, I will charitably assume that Heather must have misunderstood.'

'Must have,' Lian agreed woodenly.

Normally articulate and decisive, Jared muttered something that sounded neither, and stormed out, then had to return for the coffee. Grabbing up the mugs with so much force that hot coffee slopped over his knuckles, he marched away.

She let him get all the way into the hall before calling softly, 'Jared?'

Halting, his back ramrod-stiff, he muttered without turning, 'Yes?'

'Wouldn't it be nice if, just now and then, you could try to remember that I'm doing you a favour?'

He didn't answer, but then she hadn't really expected that he would. The study door slammed to with a resounding crash.

And so endeth the second lesson. Never underestimate your opponent.

Instead of sandwiches, she put together cold meat and salad, with not even a pinch of cyanide. Leaving them in the fridge, her face still closed, tight, she went into the lounge. Angry and hurt, her mind not entirely on what she was doing, she selected a book at random and returned to the garden. Settling herself in one of the lounge chairs Mary had put out, she opened the book and stared blindly at the print.

A spoke before the wheel was built? she wondered. No, because Heather had had no reason to suppose that the wheel ever would *be* built. She presumably had no real knowledge of the kiss they'd exchanged, or how pleasurable it had been. And how meaningless. To him, at any rate. No, it was just a case of getting rid of any woman who might prove to be a threat to her desire to win Jared for herself. But what a little bitch. To deliberately lie just because she felt threatened. Desperately threatened to behave like that. Poor Heather. Or was it poor Lian?

With a bitter little smile, she leaned back and closed her eyes. So now she really must leave—or be sacked. Anyway, she needed something that would occupy her mind to the exclusion of all else, not this drifting sort of arrangement that left too much time to brood. Such as what? she wondered drearily. She wasn't equipped to do anything else. She would miss Simon, though— and Jared. She liked him—had liked him, Lian, past tense, she insisted to herself. She'd liked other men, of course, been attracted before, including the wretched David.

Were her feelings for Jared rebound stuff? No, and in all honesty they weren't in the least like her feelings for David had been. She had always known that he'd been jealous of her success, had felt threatened by her, no matter how he tried to hide it. Most men did. Or had, she qualified to herself. Without her overriding desire, her competitive spirit, she was about as threatening as wet string. Which, she supposed, was partly why she felt so angry and frustrated. She had been whatever the feminine was for emasculated. Would Jared have been jealous of her success? Felt threatened by her? No, she didn't honestly think that he would.

'Hi, Lian.'

Opening her eyes, she stared at a very grubby Simon. There was a streak of dirt across one cheek; his hair was every which way, his T-shirt filthy, the knee of his jeans torn.

'Hi,' she greeted, still feeling dreary and confused. 'Who won?'

Not altogether familiar with irony, he gave a comical frown as he sank down beside her chair. 'What?'

'You look as though you've been in a scrap, and I wondered who won.'

'Nah,' he grinned. 'Peter and me have been building a raft.' Tying up the trailing lace of his trainers, he lay back. 'It's sports day next Friday. Coming?' he asked casually.

Not sure how to answer, because she wasn't sure if she would still be here, but not wanting to lie to him, she evaded the issue by asking, 'What are you in?'

'Sack race, obstacle, two hundred metres,' he listed offhandedly. 'It's at two o'clock. Dad still working?'

'Mm, still in the study with Heather.'

Lian pulled a face, whether for his father working, or Heather being there, she didn't know, nor enquired, although they were a similar sort of grimaces to those he had made at the breakfast table when his father had mentioned his secretary.

'So what's this about a raft?' she asked lightly.

Opening his eyes, Simon gave her a rather adult, speculative look. 'The Scouts are having a raft race next Saturday. Do you think Dad will let me go in it?'

'I didn't know you were in the Scouts.'

'I'm not, but they said anybody could go if they wanted. So, do you reckon he will?'

'I've no idea. You'll have to ask him.'

With what he presumably hoped was a winning smile, he begged, 'Couldn't you? He'll listen to you. He likes you,' he added artfully, and she knew very well that he was referring to their behaviour the night before when he'd interrupted them. Behaviour that was not likely to be repeated.

'Still not my place,' she denied mildly. 'You'll have to do your own dirty work, chum.'

'Spoil-sport.'

'Mm. Rotten old world, isn't it?'

With a laugh, Simon bounded to his feet and began to walk towards the house. 'Is it lunchtime? I'm starving!'

With a sad, rather rueful smile, she got up to follow him. 'Go and wash your hands, then tell your Dad and Heather that food is ready when they want it.'

'OK.'

Cutting up a stick of French bread, she buttered the pieces and put them in a basket. Laying knives and forks round the table, she got out the salad and condiments just as Simon returned, closely followed by Jared and Heather. Heather very carefully didn't look at her. Jared merely glanced in her direction, to see if she was chastened? she wondered. Or was he expecting an apology? If he was, he could expect till Doomsday, and still be without it.

'Oh, that looks nice,' Heather gushed prettily as she gazed at the rather depressed-looking salad.

'How kind of you to say so,' Lian replied with equal insincerity. 'You must be exhausted, do sit down and start. Simon,' she continued without pause for breath, 'have you washed your hands?'

Simon gave her a look she rightly deserved. She gave him a sweet smile, which also encompassed his father.

Jared returned it, without any humour at all. Simon giggled.

They sat around the table like actors in a very bad play, and Lian feared that she was about to copy Simon and get a fit of the giggles. Heather endeavoured to give the very misleading impression of the shy little secretary almost overwhelmed at being invited to lunch with the boss, and, as though afraid of silences that might be filled by her arch enemy, she fired a spate of questions at Simon that would have been far more suited to a five-year-old, and when she did pause for breath Simon leapt thankfully into the breach.

'Dad? Are you coming to sports day on Friday? It's at two o'clock. Lian says she'll come.'

And that's really likely to encourage him, Lian thought wryly as she gave Simon a reproving look, because she hadn't said anything of the sort.

'Friday?' he queried as though his mind wasn't really on the conversation. 'Yes, of course, don't I always?'

'And,' Simon continued, presumably, having grasped the bull by the horns, now feeling that it might be best to just hang on, 'can I take part in the raft race?'

'What raft race?' his father frowned.

'The Scouts. They're having a raft race.'

'You're not in the Scouts.'

Casting his eyes up to heaven, he repeated what he had told Lian. 'So can I go?'

'Where's it to be?'

'On the river, of course!'

'Don't be rude,' Jared reproved automatically.

'Sorry. So can I?'

'I don't know. Is it supervised?'

'Sure,' Simon said glibly.

'I'll think about it.'

'Yes, but——'

'I said,' Jared put in firmly, 'I'll think about it. Now eat your meal.'

Lapsing into a rather mutinous silence, the boy did as he was told.

And we haven't heard the last of that, Lian thought. She was right, they hadn't. The row later that afternoon, after Heather had gone home, could be heard all over the house.

'But why?' Simon demanded.

'Because you lied to me! You said it was supervised!'

'It is!'

'But not by the Scout master, or any responsible adult, which is what you knew I meant!'

'No, I didn't,' Simon denied sulkily. 'And the older boys are responsible.'

'At fifteen?' Jared asked in disbelief. 'No one that age is responsible,' he retorted, rather unfairly.

'But everyone else is going,' Simon wailed.

'That I doubt very much.'

'But it won't be dangerous or anything!' he pleaded. 'It's only on the narrow part. I——'

'No!' Jared thundered. 'I've said no, and I mean no, and if you want me to take you to the coast tomorrow will you please go away and let me work?'

Slamming out of Jared's study with enough force to shatter the door-frame, Simon stormed through the kitchen and out into the garden. 'I hate him!' he muttered. 'And I don't want to go to the rotten coast! It isn't fair!'

Standing in the open back door, Lian watched him kick furiously at one of the rocks edging the flower-bed before he stormed off towards the stream. Poor Simon.

'Where's he gone?' Jared asked from behind her. He still sounded cross, and Lian guessed that it was caused partly by guilt because he'd been impatient.

'Down to the stream, I imagine. He'll be back when he's worked off his temper.'

'Thank you so much,' he retorted sarcastically, 'but I really don't need you to explain my son's behaviour to me!'

'I wasn't,' she returned on a sigh. 'Merely making an observation.'

'Well, keep them to yourself!' he muttered pettishly. 'I am quite capable of handling my own son, and I do not need other people sticking their oars into what doesn't concern them!'

'Fine; my oars will, in future, remain firmly in their rowlocks.'

'Oh, shut up!' Turning on his heel, Jared stormed back to the study and the door received much the same abusive treatment as that meted out by his son.

Hey-ho. She would definitely be leaving, Lian decided, and the sooner the better. The thought filled her with sadness.

With nothing much else to do, she wandered down towards the wood to find Simon. He was hurling stones into the stream with the obvious wish that it was his father he was abusing. Knowing better than to even try to calm him down, she idly reached for the rope that was tucked over a nearby branch. She wasn't fool enough to try swinging on it with her injured back, but the stream was narrow enough to almost skip across, so, holding the rope for balance, she stepped across to the other side. With a faint smile at the still watching Simon, she stepped back, lost her balance on the muddy bank and slithered ignominiously into the water.

'Oh, sh——' Clamping her mouth hastily shut on what she'd been about to say, Lian gave the now hysterical boy a wry grin. Standing up to her shins in the water, her skirt soaked at the hem, she said drily, 'Well, that'll learn me, won't it? And I don't know what you're laughing at; I bet it's what you did the day I came. I remember the state you were in, even if you don't.' Extending her hand to be pulled out, she squelched up the bank and on to dry land. Sinking down on to a convenient boulder, she took off her espadrilles and emptied them. 'Feeling better now?' she asked him gently.

'I guess,' he shrugged. 'Me and Peter had already started making it; it was going to be really neat.'

'Then why not use it for something else?' she suggested.

'Like what?'

'Oh, I don't know. A tree-house?'

Staring at her, his face thoughtful while he presumably worked out the implications, the pleasures or otherwise, Simon gave a slow smile. 'Yeah.'

'Hey, where are you going?' she shouted after his rapidly disappearing form.

'I have to tell Peter!'

'Well, don't be late for tea!'

A backwards wave was the only indication she had that he'd heard her.

'Wretched boy.'

'And father?' Jared asked quietly from behind her.

CHAPTER FOUR

SWINGING round in surprise, Lian stared up at Jared.

'It all got a bit out of hand, didn't it?'

'Yes,' she agreed quietly. In more ways than one.

'I'm not usually so—difficult.' Squatting down beside her, he pulled up a blade of grass and began to chew on it. 'I've been in a filthy temper these last few days.'

'I had noticed,' she said drily.

With a faint smile, he looked at her. 'Don't bear a grudge, Lian?'

It wasn't a question of bearing a grudge, it was a question of being disappointed that he wasn't the man she thought he was, and wanting something she couldn't have. Only she couldn't say that, could she? So where was the point in being picky? 'No,' she agreed, 'I don't bear a grudge.'

'Thanks.'

'But that doesn't mean I enjoy being shouted at,' she added. 'Or accused.'

'No,' he agreed heavily. Balanced easily on his toes, without the creak of knee joints, or the shifting of muscles that usually accompanied the casual pose, he removed the stalk from his mouth and idly examined it. 'But it's a sad fact of life that those who put up with it are more likely to be shouted at than those who don't.' With a swift sideways glance he returned his attention to the grass.

'Meaning Heather would have walked out if you'd shouted at her? And you couldn't afford to have that happen, could you?'

'That makes me sound——'

'Calculating, yes. But then, you wouldn't have shouted at her, would you? Because you believed all she said.'

'I believe she *believed* what she said—a subtle difference. You can be—sharp.'

'There, and it still all ended up my fault, didn't it?' Lian asked admiringly.

With a grunt of laughter, he pointed out, 'You have to admit that you are sometimes rather provocative, and—er—disconcerting.'

'Am I?'

'Yes. Blunt, and a bit confusing for a mere male.'

'Oh, mere, is it?' she asked with a lightness that she wasn't really feeling.

'Mm.' Flicking his eyes back to hers, Jared added more seriously, 'I've had a lot on my mind. Not least of which is trying to find a damned housekeeper.'

'Yes.'

'And so, to be fair, has Heather. I've been working her pretty hard these last few days. She was obviously cross and upset at her car breaking down; maybe she goaded you,' he offered handsomely.

'Maybe,' she agreed, because how the hell did you tell a man that his secretary was a damned little liar?

Obviously convinced that the matter was now resolved, Jared leaned forward, no doubt putting one hell of a strain on his thigh muscles, and kissed her. 'How hard am I to try and find a housekeeper?' he asked with the hopeful inflexion of a man sure of his ability to charm.

'Hard,' she insisted. 'And whether goaded or not, I still didn't say those things to Heather.' She wasn't about to be caught the same way twice. Wasn't about to let things ride as she had with David. If there was one thing she had learned during the past unhappy weeks, it was to get things aired out in black and white. Her gaze steady, hoping that it hid her reaction to his brief kiss, she reproved, 'And that wasn't fair.'

'What? Kissing you? Why? You think I'm only being nice to you because I need you to look after my son?'

'Aren't you?'

'No.' Tilting her chin up, forcing her to meet his gaze, he repeated, 'No. You really think I'm that calculating?'

'I don't know.'

'But the scales would tilt toward yes rather than no?' he persisted.

'I would have to think so, yes,' she admitted.

'Not true,' he denied. Rocking back on his heels, he let his breath out in a little sigh. 'I like you, Lian. I like you very much...'

'But that's as far as it goes?' she finished for him.

'Yes,' he agreed with a look of relief. 'I enjoy your company, I enjoy sparring with you, and I would very much enjoy a flirtation with you. You're an exceptionally attractive woman, and I wouldn't be human if I wasn't affected by it. But that's all it is. I don't want a commitment, Lian—and I don't want you to be hurt. But neither would I use any feelings that are between us to further another cause.'

'Not because you need me to look after your son?'

'No.' A faint twinkle in his dark eyes, he asked, 'You don't think a man would be nice to you just because you're nice? Oh!' he exclaimed softly. 'David. Is that what this is all about? He used you, so you think all men are the same?'

Shaking her head, Lian denied it. 'No, I'm not that much of a fool.' But it had to be admitted that there were similarities between them. Or seemed to be.

'I'm very glad to hear it,' he approved, 'because I would *hate* for you to sell yourself short. You must know that any red-blooded male worth his salt would yearn to have an affair with you. Including me. Simon or no Simon.'

Evasion? Or the simple truth? But she didn't want an affair with him—she wanted more, only that would be wishing for the moon. And he still hadn't said whether he believed her—or Heather.

With a gentleness that was perhaps more hurtful than arrogance, he pleaded gently, 'Don't fall in love with me, Lian.'

Forcing herself to smile, to make her eyes amused, she shook her head. 'I wouldn't dream of it. And, by the same token, don't use me for light relief—or whipping boy,' she added pointedly.

'I wouldn't dream of it,' he parodied. 'Perhaps Heather was just feeling a bit peeved, hm?' His grin felt like a knife-thrust, but at least it meant that he believed her, didn't it? And that was balm to her pride. Pride also dictated that he never got the faintest hint of how he made her feel. 'Ten days to go, and still no housekeeper. How good are you at housework?' she quipped.

With a slow, seductive smile, his eyes alight with laughter, he murmured, 'I've had no complaints.'

'No, that I can believe,' she agreed wryly, 'and that wasn't what I meant. As you very well know.'

'Do I? Not because you were feeling domestic?' he teased with a hopeful leer.

'No.'

'Pity.'

With a reluctant laugh, she slowly extended her finger and pushed him backwards. She should have stayed cross with him—it would have been safer—but he surely didn't make it easy.

Rising easily to his feet, he held out his hand and pulled her up and into his arms. 'Don't fancy a little bit of bed-making?' he asked, tongue in cheek.

'Uh-uh,' she denied.

'Lounge-lazing?'

Her head on one side as she stared up into his humorous face, Lian gave a rueful smile. 'You make it very hard to stay angry with you.'

'That was the idea. You were thinking of leaving, weren't you?'

'Yes,' she admitted honestly.

'And now?'

'I don't know,' she sighed. 'I have to go soon. I can't stay here forever.'

'But not today,' he persuaded softly. 'And you wouldn't want to miss sports day, now would you?'

'Wouldn't I?'

'No.' Moving her to his side, Jared linked his fingers in hers and led her towards the garden, and the welcome shade of a large tree. Seating himself on the springy turf, he patted the ground beside him.

She was being a fool, weak-willed; she should say no and mean it. Allowing herself to be persuaded into talking with him, laughing with him was tantamount to an admission that she was willing to have an affair. So have an affair, she told herself impatiently. It would be something nice to remember. He was probably a terrific lover... And he might fall in love with her, mightn't he? Oh, don't be so wet! All this was doing was delaying the inevitable. But she still sat down. Spreading her wet skirt tidily over her legs, she leaned back against the tree.

With a pleasurable sigh, he shuffled round and laid his head in her lap. Picking up her hand, he placed it in the open neck of his shirt. 'Tell me about you,' he commanded softly. 'Have you always wanted to be a sailor?'

Not quite sure if she was exasperated or amused, Lian idly traced his strong features, smoothed back his thick, unruly hair, and there was both pleasure and pain in her actions, a funny little ache in her insides. 'You really aren't being fair,' she murmured quietly.

'Yes, I am, I'm stopping you doing something you'll ultimately regret.' Giving her a quizzical smile, he encouraged, 'Now tell me.'

Manipulation pure and simple, but it was a gentle manipulation, one which she wasn't quite strong enough to refuse, and perhaps talking about it might ease that particular ache at least. Her face thoughtful, she gazed back into the past.

'Since the age of thirteen, when my mother died, and Dad and I went down to stay with his sister in Devon, I have wanted to sail. Devon was different from anything we had ever known, and we both fell in love with it. So much so that Dad gave up his job, sold the house in London, bought a cottage not far from Exmouth—and we both discovered the pleasure to be had from messing about on the water. The freedom, the challenge. At every available opportunity we would make for the shore, beg tuition, talk to sailors. We took to it like the proverbial ducks.'

'And progressed from there to the bigger yachts? No, don't stop, that's nice,' Jared encouraged when her hand momentarily halted its soothing movements over his hair.

Threading her fingers through the thick strands, enjoying it as much as he, she continued, 'I did; Dad preferred the smaller craft, but me? Oh, me, I wanted to be bigger and better than anyone else. I'm very competitive,' she told him with a smile, just in case he hadn't noticed. 'I don't know why, just the way I'm made, I suppose.'

'And made very nicely,' he smiled. 'And, now that you can no longer be bigger and better, what will you do instead? When you leave here?' he asked gently.

He made it sound so definite, her leaving. No hope there. But had she ever thought there was? 'I don't know,' she sighed. 'I really do not know.' Determinedly pushing aside her troubles, she asked, 'Tell me about you. Were you brought up round here?'

'Mm, a Victorian monstrosity across the other side of the town.'

'Was that where your father died?'

'Yes.'

'But you didn't want to live there?' she persisted. Dear heaven, it was like getting blood out of a stone. Stubborn, humorous, easy to talk to—he chatted and said nothing.

'No, no way did I ever want to live there again. When he died, I put it up for sale. I wasn't intending then to stay and run the works. I'd been living and working in Canada,' he explained quietly, 'but when Simon was nearly five, coming up to school age, we returned to England. I bought a house near Kendal because I like that part of the country, and assumed, I suppose, that I would stay there until Simon was grown up. Only it didn't work out that way. I couldn't leave him there while I came down to sort the works out, could I? I'm all he's got, poor chap, and to uproot him from school and his friends seemed damned unfair, but what choice did I have? I still don't know if I did the right thing. First Nan dying, and now this. I *know* what I should be doing for him; it's just finding the damned time. He needs far more attention than I'm able to give him at present.'

'And as soon as you finish here you'll go back to Kendal?'

'Yes.'

'You never thought of marrying again?'

'For Simon's sake?'

'No,' she denied, 'for yours.'

'No, I don't think I will ever marry again.'

'Not even Heather?'

'Heather?' he exclaimed in astonishment. 'Good God, no. You do have a bee in your bonnet about that, don't you? I'm fond of her, she's a very good secretary, but anything further? No.'

Poor Heather. Didn't he know how she felt about him? Or was his vehemence because he did? And why was he so convinced that he would never remarry? Because his wife would be such a hard act to follow? 'What was she like, your wife?' she asked with a sort of morbid curiosity.

'Penny?' A smile in his eyes as he stared up at the overlapping branches above them, he said eventually, 'Sweet. God, that sounds awful, but she was. I don't think I ever heard her say a bad word about anyone;

never heard her complain. Gentle and sweet. It seems such a long time ago. Another life.' Focusing back on her face, he abruptly changed the subject. 'Are you still intending to go back to Devon?'

'I don't know. Probably.'

'You wouldn't—um—consider staying around here?' he asked lightly.

'For what reason?'

'You know for what reason. Don't you?'

'Yes,' she admitted, 'but it wouldn't work.' Wouldn't it? The trouble was, one sign from him, the right sign, and she was beginning to think it would work only too well. Only there wouldn't be a sign, would there? In which case she had to give him a concrete reason for her refusal. 'I need the sea, I told you.'

'Because it's necessary to your well-being—and because you're a lady who doesn't go in for half-measures,' he commented quietly. 'You gave your all to the sea, didn't you? Put all your eggs in one basket.'

'Yes, and now I don't know what I am, or what I want to do.'

'No.' With a comforting smile, Jared lifted his hand and rubbed his thumb gently across her lower lip. 'There's no one special in your life at the moment?'

'No.' But there was. The man lying with his head in her lap was special, or beginning to be, and that really wouldn't do. More heartache she just couldn't face.

'Good.' Rolling to the side, he drew her down to lean over him, then tucked her hand against his shoulder. 'Stop looking so solemn,' he urged. 'It's a nice day, I'm with a nice lady—and you promised me some lawn-lazing.'

'I did?' Staring down into his face, Lian felt her stomach curl, felt excitement and alarm buzz along her veins. This was stupid. This was really asking for trouble, especially when he seemed to take her hesitation for provocation. Before she could object, stop him, he moved into a more easily accessible position, framed her face with his palms, and raised his head in order to touch his mouth to hers. 'It isn't a commitment, Lian, a desire for it to lead to other things, just a pleasurable moment out of time.'

And that was supposed to reassure her? It might be a pleasurable moment out of time for him, but for her? Yet was she really sure that she was falling in love with him? Might it not be just the need for some warmth? Because she'd been hurt? And was still vulnerable? And at the moment she was quite in control. Wasn't she? Still thinking with her mind? And she did want him to kiss her. Wanted to know if it could affect her as it had previously.

Before her mental deliberations were even halfway completed, he had drawn her mouth back to his, and there *was* the same feeling as before, the same warmth, that delicious surge of pleasure in her stomach, and when he deepened the kiss she abandoned her reasoning altogether. She could have said no. Could have stopped him, she hazily assured herself, but the truth was she didn't want to. She wanted to have his arms round her, his mouth exploring hers. Wanted to feel needed, loved.

Without them quite expecting it, pleasure eased into passion; desire into need; languor into urgency and Jared half rolled to the side so that her body fitted his exactly. Curve to curve, convex to concave; and, needing more, she urged him over on to his back, kept her body tight to his, moved slightly to accommodate his arousal, and breathing and heartbeat accelerated as she returned his kisses as she had never returned them with anyone before.

'I want you,' he husked thickly, his brown eyes almost black as he gazed into her eyes. 'And at any moment Simon is likely to erupt into the garden, demanding to be fed, played with, assisted with some great plan, and I'm damned if I'm going to scramble guiltily to rearrange clothing that is disarranged, pretend an insouciance I am very far from feeling.'

'No,' Lian agreed equally thickly, her breathing laboured. Slightly resentful that he could be so in control, when she appeared to have no control at all, she stared into his eyes and fought to regain her sanity.

'So will you please roll, very carefully, to one side,' he continued huskily, 'before the urge to give in becomes too great to control?'

'Yes.' Desire still vivid in her lovely eyes, despite her efforts to dispel it, she moved not a muscle.

'Lian?' he queried, and then his own eyes widened in alarm. With a grunt of laughter, he shoved her one way, rolled the other and lay face down, his hands folded beneath his cheek, just as Simon and Peter emerged from behind the shrubbery.

Sprawled inelegantly, her skirt rucked up round her thighs, Lian stared at them in consternation, then gave a wry, if somewhat shaky smile. They were chattering animatedly, and took not a blind bit of notice of the two under the tree. It was a moot point whether they even saw them.

Jared was still shaking with laughter, and she thumped him resentfully on the back.

Turning his head towards her, his face full of humour, he grinned. 'I told you we should have gone indoors.' Peering across her, he queried in surprise, 'Now where have they gone?'

'Into the barn.'

'For how long, one wonders?' With a teasing smile, seeming not to notice Lian's withdrawal, Jared slid one hand across her stomach, then snatched it back quickly and shut his eyes as the barn door was flung noisily open.

Simon came to stand beside her, a broad grin on his face. 'Hi.'

'Hi yourself,' she managed, then found that she needed to clear her throat before she could resume. 'Hello, Peter,' she added with a smile for the fair-haired boy. He looked shy, and rather sweet, and she wondered how much trouble he managed to get himself into with a friend like Simon around.

'Hello,' he mumbled.

'Dad asleep?' Simon asked as he eyed his father's recumbent form.

'Yes, he's been snoring for hours.'

'He doesn't snore! Does he?'

'No. Joke. Did you want him for something?'

'No, no,' he denied airily, 'just wondered. Come on, Peter.'

'Now where are you off to?'

'Oh, nowhere, just down to the woods.' Giving his friend a shove in the right direction, they raced off towards the stream.

'And I recognised *that* tone,' Jared said as he cautiously opened his eyes and raised his head. 'Up to no good and no mistake!'

'Probably,' she agreed with quiet abstraction as she watched the two boys disappear.

'No probably about it.' Rolling on to his back, he laced his hands beneath his neck. 'I don't feel like cooking, do you?'

'No,' she denied quietly.

'Fancy a walk down to the pub? They do a reasonable meal.'

'Sounds good,' she managed evenly.

'Right.' Levering himself reluctantly to his feet, Jared stood looking down at her for a moment, then smiled. 'You look delightfully abandoned, Miss Grayson.'

'I *have* been abandoned!' she informed him without quite meeting his eyes. 'At the height of my passion, too!'

'Now don't start,' he warned mock sternly. 'You *cannot* have your wicked way with me. Not yet, anyway. However, after a few drinks...'

'Think I ought to get you drunk?' Dear God, how could she act when she felt so bewildered and bereft?

'No-o, I think you ought to get me mellow.' Extending his hand to her, he pulled her to her feet. 'Go and get showered and changed, because I am *not* taking you out looking like that! I'll go and find the hounds.'

Not sure whether she should be profoundly thankful, or profoundly resentful that he did not seem to notice her agitation, Lian forced herself to stroll slowly into the house just as someone began pounding on the front door. Oh, God, now what? Walking across to answer it, she stared in query at a middle-aged lady holding a sheaf of papers. 'Miss Grayson?'

'Yes,' Lian admitted in surprise.

Much to her astonishment, the woman nodded in a satisfied sort of way, and declared warmly, 'Yes, you'll do.' Thrusting the papers at her, she retorted, 'I am fed up with trying to get hold of him, and of trying to fax things to him when his wretched machine obviously doesn't work! And will you kindly tell him that this rural solitude he's indulging in is playing havoc with his business? And those,' she continued irascibly, prodding the papers, 'he'll have to deal with himself, because I am going home! I think I'm coming down with this damned flu.' As if to prove it, she sneezed. Turning, she began to walk back down the path.

'But who are you?' Lian called after her.

Halting, she gave Lian a look of astonishment. 'His secretary. From London,' she added. 'Oh, and you can tell him that Davies still isn't back.'

Davies? Who the hell was Davies? And why would she do? For what? Still frowning, Lian watched the woman get into a small red car. Closing the door, she continued to stare thoughtfully at it for a moment. Another London secretary? Glancing idly down at the papers, she read the heading across the top one. Lowe Enterprises. Enterprises? What enterprises? He'd said he was an engineer. Just who the hell was Jared Lowe? Chewing thoughtfully on her lower lip, recalling, belatedly, some odd snippets of conversation she'd overheard, about money transfers, properties, she began to wonder again just how important he was. Surely an engineer didn't need two secretaries? And a London office? Curious, and checking to make sure that Jared was nowhere in sight, she walked into the study and picked up the phone. Clive would know. Clive knew everything. A freelance journalist who had once, not so very long ago, worked on the City desk of a reputable newspaper.

'Clive? It's Lian.'

'Lian!' he exclaimed warmly. 'Darling girl, how are you? Sorry to hear about your troubles.'

'Never mind my troubles,' she said dismissively. 'But thanks,' she added belatedly. 'Clive, have you ever heard of a Jared Lowe?'

'Well, of course I have, sweetie.'

'You have?' she asked in surprise.

'Yes. Everyone's heard of Jared Lowe.'

'Oh. Well, who is he?'

'You mean you don't know?'

'Clive! If I knew I'd hardly be asking you, would I?'

'No, I suppose not. He's head of Lowe Enterprises. Very, very full of juice, duckie.'

'I do wish you wouldn't talk in that affected way!' she reproved, irritable without quite knowing why. 'This is me, remember? The girl whose pigtails you pulled in junior school.' Very full of juice? she pondered. He wasn't hard up, she knew that, but wealthy? Might not be the same Jared Lowe, of course. 'What does he look like?'

'Tall, dark hair and eyes, dresses like one of his workforce instead of the multi-millionaire he undoubtedly is. Escorts beautiful women to various functions—or did,' he qualified. 'No one seems to have seen much of him over the last year.'

'No. Oh, well, thanks, Clive.' Replacing the receiver, Lian stood frowning down at it for a minute, then turned and saw Jared leaning in the doorway. He looked amused.

'You lied to me,' she accused.

'I did? When?'

'When you said... Did... Well, by omission,' she muttered confusedly. 'Which means that Jared Lowe, multi-millionaire, of Lowe Enterprises, whatever they are, does not need someone like me to drive him around. Does he? In fact he probably has a fleet of chauffeurs!'

'No,' he denied mildly. 'Only one.'

'Then where is he?'

'Flu,' he said sadly.

Severely repressing her irritation, she asked loftily, 'And the housekeeper? You could call in an army of people to take care of Simon, couldn't you?'

'No one he likes,' he murmured blandly. 'He likes you. And Mary, of course.'

'I knew I was being manipulated,' she muttered. 'I *knew* that. I just didn't know how much.'

'Money doesn't necessarily mean you can find the person you want,' he reproved softly.

'No, but it gives you a hell of a wider choice. Doesn't it?'

'True. And now that you know I'm a millionaire, does it make a difference?' he asked in the same soft voice.

'I don't know, do I?'

With a laugh, he walked slowly across, and bent to kiss her. 'Good girl.'

Eyeing him sardonically, she accused, 'You don't look like a millionaire.'

'No, so I've been told. But what, my dear Miss Grayson, does one actually look like?'

Thinking about it, a rueful smile lit her eyes. 'Silly question.'

'Mm, almost as silly as your accusation. So what prompted this little fact-finding episode?' he asked lightly.

'What…? Oh.' Looking round for the papers she'd dumped down when she rang Clive, Lian picked them up and handed them to him. 'A lady came, said she was your London secretary. She also said that I would do! What does that mean?'

'I've no idea,' Jared denied even more blandly. 'Anything else?'

'Yes! She said she was going home and that you would have to deal with those,' she instructed with a little nod towards the papers he held. 'She thought she was coming down with flu. She also complained about your fax machine not working; said Davies wasn't back… Davies being?'

'My chauffeur.'

'Right; why are you grinning?'

'Thoughts, Miss Grayson, just thoughts.'

'Hm. So now tell me who you are.'

A smile still playing about his mouth, he explained briefly, 'Lowe Enterprises is me, I suppose. It involves a—er—vast amount of property. Shops, houses, businesses. Normally there is very little for me to do; it's managed very ably by a group of people, one of whom is Miss Gentle, my personal secretary. My right arm, in fact—— Damn!' he suddenly broke off to exclaim. 'I need her! Was she sure it was flu?'

'Yes,' Lian said firmly, 'and stop prevaricating.'

'Sorry,' he sighed, his mind more obviously on the sickness of Miss Gentle than on her. 'Normally I only have to attend board meetings and the like, sign a few papers.'

More than that, she suspected, but still. 'Go on.'

'Hm? Oh, well, due to the recession, people having to make cut-backs, businesses going to the wall, I've had to make some decisions.'

He said it as though he didn't really know what decisions were, and Lian wondered if this under-playing of his abilities was the reason he had become a millionaire.

'I've had to decide how much licence to give the people who rent the properties, whether to wait in the hope that things will pick up, whether to sell, buy. It's a knock-on effect—what affects one, often affects all. In varying degrees. Usually things trundle along pretty smoothly because I have an excellent work-force to take care of all the day-to-day running of the company, but due to this damned flu bug, with half my management team out sick, I'm having to take a more active part. And, coming right in the middle of this business at the engineering works, life has got decidedly complicated.'

Smiling at her derisive expression, he added, 'All inherited wealth, Lian, nothing I can take much credit for. It all belonged to my mother's family. Sadly, the cousin who should have inherited died in his teens.'

'So, not expecting to inherit, you became an engineer.'

'Yes. Now go on up and get changed.'

With a mock salute, she went upstairs, her mind filled with thoughts of Jared. Half-truth, half-evasion, she decided. Jared was not the sort of man to take a back seat in any business. He had an enquiring mind, a forceful personality, and he would want his finger very firmly in every pie. The knowledge that he was a millionaire didn't particularly worry her; after all, she'd mixed with all sorts of people—the yachting

fraternity were made up of the poor and hopeful, the
rich and famous, even royalty. No, what did worry
her was the fact that Jared had access to very many
and beautiful women. Why? she derided herself
crossly. What damn difference does that make? You
knew he didn't want you, only for a bit of light dalliance. Yes, but all the time she hadn't known about
the other beautiful women there was a chance, wasn't
there? A chance for what? she asked herself scornfully. For him to fall in love with a penniless ex-captain
of a yacht? When he could have his pick of society?
And, being wealthy to boot, they'd be falling all over
him, wouldn't they? Kicking irritably at the wall, she
stalked into the bathroom.

You shouldn't have let him kiss you again. No. You
shouldn't have kissed him back. No. Because now you
know what you're going to be missing instead of only
imagining. It wasn't fair. And you only have yourself
to blame. Wrenching on the lever of the shower with
nearly enough force to break it, she stripped off and
stood resolutely beneath the cool jets. No more. See
the week out, go to sports day, and then leave. Right.

When she'd showered, and clad in a peach satin
camisole and knickers, she sat miserably on the bed
and brushed out her long hair. He'd wanted her to
stay for Simon's sake, not his, and she'd known that.
Always known that. Self-deception is a terrible thing,
Lian. But how on earth had it happened so fast? One
moment she was miserable, bitter and confused, and
the next tumbling headlong into love with Jared Lowe.
Now wait a minute, not really love—attraction . . . All
right, severe attraction . . . The knock on the door was
only half heard, and before she could react it opened.

'You left your shoes . . . Oh, sorry, Lian.'

Staring at him, only half registering the fact that he was actually in her room, and that she was half naked, she gave Jared a distracted smile. 'Shoes? Oh, right, thanks.' Holding out her hand for them, she took the water-stiffened canvas from him, and then realised, belatedly, how she must appear. Her robe was in the bathroom, her dress hanging on the wardrobe; there was nothing in fact to wrap herself in, apart from the duvet, and he would think . . .

'Dear God,' he said softly, 'but you are an astonishingly beautiful woman.'

'No . . .' she began.

'Yes.' As though he wasn't truly aware of what he was doing, he walked across to her, perched on the other side of the bed, and picked up a handful of her long hair.

Stiffening, not sure what to do for the best, she left it too late. With a gentle tug, he pulled her backwards so that she sprawled across the bed. With his other hand he smoothed the soft material of her camisole across her ribs. And she let him. 'Beautiful,' he murmured before bending and capturing her mouth with his.

He smelled of soap, tasted of toothpaste; his palm was warm through the silk of her top, and heat spread through her. She wanted him, dear God, how she wanted him. Wanted to wrap her long legs round him; wanted his hands to roam. With a deep, shaky breath, horrified that she could forget her resolutions so quickly, Lian held him at bay and stared shakily up into his dark, dark eyes.

'Since the very first time your eyes smiled at me, I've wanted you,' Jared said quietly. 'Wanted you in my bed.'

'No!' she exclaimed, her voice strangled.

'Yes. Wanted...'

'Dad?' a faintly worried voice queried from the landing. 'Where are you?'

Letting all his breath out on a long sigh, he gave a rueful smile. '"For whom the bell tolls"...' Dropping one last swift kiss on her parted mouth, he got up and walked quietly out.

Releasing her own breath, she hugged her arms round her. She could still taste his mouth, feel his warmth, and heat flooded through her. With a groan of despair, she sat up. I can't handle this, she told herself shakily. Then don't think! Just hold yourself together long enough to get dressed, walk down to the pub with them, and then explain quietly, rationally that you are leaving. And never see him again? Yes. Never see him again! But that isn't what I want... Closing her eyes in despair, she forced herself to her feet. Unhooking her pink linen dress from the wardrobe, she put it on. Refusing to think, knowing that it was the only way she was going to cope with this, as she had after the accident, but for different reasons, she rewound her hair. Piling it on top of her head, she secured it with a Japanese-style stick. It was still too hot for much make-up—not that she usually wore a great deal—so she slicked mascara on to her long, dark lashes with a hand that refused to stop shaking, outlined her mouth in pink lipstick, slipped her feet into dark pink high-heeled sandals, and went to find the others. She felt all trembly inside. But determined.

Her hand linked into Jared's arm, at his insistence—another torture—Simon racing on ahead, they walked silently along the lane to collect Peter, whom Jared had invited to join them, then the half-mile into the tiny village. Well, Lian supposed that one general store-cum-post office, a pub and a garage constituted a village; if it didn't, she didn't know what else to call it. They went straight into the dining-room to eat, then sat in the garden with their drinks while the boys went to investigate the climbing-frame at the end of the small garden.

'You're very quiet,' he commented.

'Am I? Sorry,' she apologised automatically. 'I was just thinking.'

'About what?'

'Oh, this and that,' she said evasively, and was then angry with herself. She had never evaded issues before, had always met them head-on, and now was no time to fight shy. She had to tell him. For her own peace of mind. To leave it would be to make it worse. Looking down, she absently twisted her glass to and fro. 'All my life,' she began, 'I've been strong, known what I wanted and gone after it, and now I can't seem to come to terms with not being anything, and I know I agreed to stay for a bit, but, oh, Jared, I don't think I can!'

'Why? What suddenly brought this on?'

'Not suddenly,' she mumbled. God, she was doing this all wrong, but now that she'd started she had to follow it through. 'The thought of being stuck in the country with nothing to do but housework and cooking has always filled me with horror,' she explained weakly. 'And to go on, even if only for a short while, would drive me mad. I know myself well enough to know that I need something to occupy my mind, my energies...' Her energy that would far outstrip her need to be careful about her injured back.

Her energy that she would now need to outstrip her
thoughts and need of Jared. Clenching her fingers
tight on the glass, she looked away.

'And what about Simon?'

'He'll be all right,' she said without much
conviction.

'Will he? Or will he think it's his fault? I know you
said he boasted that no one would stay, but it wasn't
boasting, Lian, it was fear of rejection. Get in first
before they have a chance to.'

'But he didn't like any of them!' she protested.

'Maybe, probably because he was comparing them
all with Nan. You aren't in the least like Nan, and he
likes you very much. So what do you think that will
do to him if you leave? The first person he liked . . .'

'Oh, that's not fair! I told you both right from the
start that I wouldn't stay.'

'I'm never fair where my son's welfare is concerned, and you promised me two weeks! A car is
being delivered for your use tomorrow; that will give
you some independence . . .'

'It has nothing to do with independence!'

'Then what has it to do with?'

You, she wanted to shout. Only how could she? He
would be astonished. He thought her worldly wise,
experienced . . . Needing a distraction, she turned her
head to watch a car pull into the car park. It was
towing a trailer holding a small sailing dinghy, and
such a wave of desolation washed over that she wanted
to weep. Not for the sailing—that, extraordinarily,
seemed to have taken second place—but as a focus
for her anguish. Couldn't she have anything in this
world that she wanted? And if that wasn't self-pity . . .
Lowering her eyes, so that he would not see her pain,

she stared into her drink. Forcing her mind away from him, she deliberately considered the forthcoming race. Probed her feelings. They'd be working up now; out practising, ironing out all the last minute wrinkles ... Jared's warm hand covering hers made her jump.

'Oh, Lian,' he said gently as he moved his eyes from the trailer to her anguished face. 'I wish there was something I could do, or say, that would make it all better. But there isn't.'

Oh, God, she didn't deserve that, did she? His kindness, his thoughtful gesture, and if he only knew the real reason for her anguish... Forcing a smile that was a travesty of her usual one, she gave in to the cowardly impulse to let him think what he would. You're a mess, Lian. Yeah. Quickly finishing her drink, she said huskily, 'I'm going to take a slow walk back. You don't mind?'

'No, you go on, we'll catch up with you later.'

Knowing that if she didn't get away, like now, she was going to do something really stupid, like cry, she hurried out of the garden. At that moment she almost hated herself. For being stupid, for being unfair to Jared, and for contemplating hurting Simon, who didn't deserve to be hurt. But how did you stop the feelings? Head down, she began to walk back to the house. And yet maybe, just maybe, the smell and taste of the sea, the wind in her hair would do what Jared had managed to do—make her forget. One to cancel out the other—and having neither. Slamming her hand angrily on to the fence beside her, she hurried on, trying to outstrip her thoughts, her feelings.

Unable to get in, because Jared had the keys, she sat on the doorstep. Her chin in her hands, she made a determined effort to be positive. She would leave, she must. But to do what? Apart from a weakness in her back, she had her health, her mind... The trouble was, schoolwork, qualifications had always taken second place to her sailing, because that was *all* she had ever wanted to do. She had some O Levels, a couple of As, but what else could she *do*? She didn't think she could bear to work in an office, even supposing she could have found a job in one. Gardening was out, because it involved a lot of bending, ditto nursery work. Coastguard? Lifeboat-woman? Lighthouse keeper? Wife and mother?

When Jared and Simon strolled into view, she was still hunched on the doorstep, deep in her own misery. Glancing up, she gave them a small smile.

Jared didn't try to persuade her to stay; perhaps he hoped that if he ignored the problem it would go away, that she would just carry on as normal.

She didn't accompany them to the coast the next day, with the excuse that she had a headache. She felt rotten and guilty when Simon looked bitterly disappointed, but he had to get used to it, didn't he? She had half intended to leave while they were gone, and then decided she couldn't. She had to tell Simon herself—and then found she couldn't when he came back laughing and happy to tell her about his day. Tomorrow, she promised herself.

Only the next day also proved impossible. Something had obviously gone very seriously wrong with matters at the works, because when Jared came home he was tight-lipped and exceedingly short-tempered. Even the mildest query got your head snapped off. And she didn't honestly think it had anything to do with her decision to leave. He seemed, conveniently, to have forgotten all about that, but she found she didn't have the heart to burden him with yet another problem. So she kept quiet. And anyway, with Jared at his most impossible, it was almost easy to pretend that she had been mistaken in her feelings for him. And then the car turned up for her use, and it would have seemed the height of bad manners to have thrown that gesture back in his face.

On the Tuesday, still making excuses to herself, and still without having told Simon, she decided to walk down to the school to meet him. He always, but always came home along the river walk with Peter. So what did he do? On the one day she had ever gone to meet him he went the other way, of course, along the road. She hung about the school for half an hour, finally made enquiries, worried herself half sick, thinking something had happened to him, and ran all the way home.

Flinging open the back door, she yelled breathlessly, 'Simon?'

A funny little squeal, followed by a thump greeted her. Pushing into the hall, nearly falling over his satchel, which was dumped in the middle of the floor, she saw the study door open. Halting in the open doorway, seeing Simon on his knees before the safe, she demanded, 'What the devil are you doing?'

Swinging guiltily round, he flushed. 'I was just trying to shut it.'

'But it shouldn't be open!'

'No,' he agreed in a small voice.

'Oh, God!' she exclaimed wearily. 'Don't say we've had burglars? I've only been gone an hour. I went to meet you.'

'Peter's Mum picked us up in the car. Oh, Lian, I can't get it shut. Dad'll do his pieces!'

'You opened it?' she asked in astonishment.

'Yeah. Only to see if I could!' he added hurriedly. 'I haven't taken anything!' Scrambling to his feet, he stood hopefully in front of her. 'You won't tell him, will you?'

'Oh, Simon!' she exclaimed weakly. 'You'll be the death of me. No, I won't tell him—if we can get it shut, that is. But how the hell did you get it open?'

Withdrawing one hand from behind his back, he sheepishly held up a piece of bent wire.

Taking it from him, Lian stared at it in some be-musement. What had Jared said? He'd probably end up in a life of crime? 'You'd better show me how you got it open, then see if we can't shut it the same way.'

Eager now to make reparation, Simon explained what he had done. 'So if you just poke it back in and twiddle it should release the lock so that you can shut it.'

'*I* poke it back in? *I* shut it?' Moving him to one side, she bent down and inserted the wire in the lock. She didn't see Simon tiptoe out, grab his satchel and hurry upstairs. Neither did she hear the front door open. The first she knew of Jared's return was his cold voice from behind her.

'And what, might I ask, do you think you're doing?'

With a little shriek of alarm, she lost her balance and fell over backwards. Looking up at his angry and disbelieving face, she gave him a small, hopeful smile, much the same as Simon had given her.

'Well?'

'It was open,' she explained with complete truth. 'I was trying to shut it.'

'Really?'

'Yes, Jared, really!' Scrambling to her feet, she held out the piece of wire. 'And if you're about to accuse me of rifling your safe don't, because I wasn't.'

'Weren't you?' Looking suddenly weary and fed up, he removed the wire from her hand, and said quietly, 'If you wanted to know anything about me, you only had to ask. I have some papers to go through,' he concluded dismissively.

With a long sigh, she went out. Another inauspicious moment to finalise her leaving plans. She didn't suppose he really thought she'd been snooping; he'd just been tired and irritable, needing someone to vent his frustration on. Hadn't he?

On the Wednesday, due, he explained shortly, to the fact that it was bloody impossible to concentrate in the office with the phones constantly ringing, Heather came to the house to work. Or was it because he didn't trust her not to go through his safe? Lian wondered when he remained somewhat distant with her. The matter hadn't been mentioned again—no apology, nor further accusation—and Lian, having promised Simon she wouldn't tell, could hardly bring it up in case further explanations were called for. Explanations she couldn't provide. And she couldn't tell him she was leaving with Heather there, could she?

'I'm expecting an important phone call,' he told both girls, 'from a Brian Haig. Whichever of you happens to answer the phone, either ensure that I speak with him immediately, or if I'm not here for some reason make sure you get his number so that I can call him back. And for God's sake be nice to him.'

Heather gave him a look that clearly said she was always nice; Lian didn't bother. And, Heather, perhaps deciding that being nasty to Lian hadn't got her anywhere, decided to be pleasant. She even apologised for her former behaviour.

Always prepared to take people on trust, Lian behaved the same; anyway, she would be leaving soon, and they were unlikely ever to meet again. Leaving them to work, she wandered out into the garden.

They worked solidly in the study till three, when Jared walked out into the kitchen where Lian was attempting to make some cakes. He still looked tired and frustrated.

'I can't think straight any more,' he explained tiredly. 'I'm going for a walk to get some fresh air and stretch my legs. Make Heather some tea, will you?'

'Sure.' Abandoning her culinary efforts, which was probably the best idea she'd had all day, she made the tea and took it through. Both phones were ringing, and Heather snatched them both up. She looked tight-lipped and irritable. With a curt order to ring back to the caller on one phone, she briefly listened to the other, 'No, no, I don't. Goodbye. Honestly, why do the damned phones always have to ring at the same time?'

'Because they're like buses,' Lian quipped, forcing a friendly tone into her voice. 'Either none at all, or they all come along together. Here, I brought you some tea.'

'Oh, thanks,' Heather said, gratefully accepting the cup. Wriggling her stiff shoulders, she tutted when the phone rang again.

'Oh, God. Answer that, will you?' she pleaded. 'I really must go to the loo.'

'Yes, of course—— Hello? What? Oh, yes, yes, it's fine. Thank you. Bye.'

With a little confused shake of her head, she replaced the receiver and returned to the kitchen.

'Anything important?' Heather called as she came downstairs.

'No, it was the telephone engineer making a line check,' she called back. Staring at her cake mixture, which sat rather lumpily in its tin, she wondered whether it was actually worth cooking it. Oh, what the hell; be brave, Lian—just because it didn't look right didn't mean it wouldn't taste it. Opening the oven, she popped it inside. Checking the time, and making a mental note to remove it at four forty-five, she turned her attention to the major decision of what to have for the evening meal. God, how did people do this day in, day out?

When Jared returned, looking no better for his stint in the fresh air, she made more tea and took it through. She heard the phone ring again, and hoped it wasn't the engineer; having to waste time answering that call would improve his temper wonderfully. Dragging out the bag of potatoes, she dumped some in a bowl of water and began to scrape them half-heartedly.

'Lian?' she heard Jared roar. Oh, hell, now what?

Wiping her hands, she trundled back to the study. 'Yes?'

'Come in here, would you, please?'

Oh, Gawd, he sounded like her old headmaster. With a little sigh, she walked inside.

'Sit down,' he ordered peremptorily.

Lian sat.

'A few minutes ago, the office rang to say that Brian Haig had rung; he had, apparently, been unable to get me on this number.' Tapping the telephone for

emphasis, just in case she didn't get the point, presumably, he resumed, 'Jackie, on the switchboard,
naturally surprised that he had been unable to do so,
fortunately, and efficiently, took his number, and I
have just rung him back.'

Bully for you. Glancing at Heather, who shrugged,
Lian wondered where the hell all this was leading. She
didn't have long to wait to find out.

'I apologised for the fact that he had been unable
to find me, and explained that I had been working at
home. Yes, he said, and, I quote, "I rang your home
and a young lady answered. She was extremely short
and denied having any knowledge of your where-
abouts."' Leaning back in his chair, Jared waited.

Leaning back in her own chair, so did Lian.

'Well?' he demanded. 'Did I, or did I not, mention
the fact that a Brian Haig might ring, and if he did
so, that you were to be polite?'

'You did,' she agreed.

'Then why the hell weren't you?'

'Presumably because I did not speak to him.'

'Didn't?' he queried pokily, 'Then perhaps you can
explain to me how the phone came to be answered
when neither you, nor Heather, did so?'

'I can't. But if it's to be a toss-up between the pair
of us, I'm to be the patsy, is that it?'

With a heavy sigh, he thumped forward in his chair
and leaned his elbows on the desk. 'Did you take a
call today?' he asked wearily.

'No.'

Turning only his head, he asked Heather, 'Did she?'

Looking embarrassed, Heather nodded. 'She said
it was the telephone engineer.'

CHAPTER FIVE

HANDS shoved into her jeans pockets, Lian glared at the stream. Your own fault, Lian, you shouldn't have made an enemy out of her, she chastised herself. No. Neither should she have stayed. But knowing both those things didn't lessen the hurt. It would make it easier to leave, though, wouldn't it?

'Lian?'

Turning her head, she stared down at Simon.

'Are you OK?'

'Sure. Just a bit fed up, don't take any notice.'

'Is it because of yesterday?'

'Yesterday?' she queried blankly.

'Yes, the safe.'

'Oh, no.'

''Cos I'll tell him if you want me to,' he offered, not very enthusiastically, it had to be admitted.

With a faint smile, she shook her head. 'How's the tree-house project going?'

It was his turn to look blank, and then he grinned. 'Oh, OK. Come and see.'

When he scampered off towards the barn, she slowly followed.

'We've got most of it nailed together,' he enthused as Lian stared at the large structure composed of odd bits of wood nailed rather inexpertly to each other.

'But how on earth will you get it into a tree?' she asked, puzzled. 'I mean, wouldn't it have been better to construct it up there?'

'Oh, we'll haul it up on a rope,' he explained breezily.

'Not in one piece,' she denied with a grin. 'One yank and half those nails will fall out.'

Staring at his handiwork, a small frown on his face, Simon reluctantly nodded. 'Yeah.'

'Don't you think it might be better to pull out some of the more bent ones?' she offered cautiously. She had no wish to hurt his obvious pride in his project, but it would be a shame to have it fall to pieces before they'd even got it into the tree.

'Mm,' he agreed thoughtfully. 'Will you help?'

'If you like,' she found herself offering, then bit her lip. Wouldn't it be kinder in the long run to be a bit distant with him? Only she found that she didn't have the heart. How could you be distant with a boy as endearing and openly enthusiastic as Simon?

'Great. Will you make a start while I go and get changed?' Grabbing up his satchel, he zoomed off.

Picking up the claw-hammer, she began to ease out the more disastrous of the nails. She would help him with this, then she would tell him she was leaving.

When he returned, dressed in his jeans and a T-shirt, they worked companionably on, until his father began bellowing for her.

With a long sigh, Lian opened the barn door and looked out. Jared was standing in the back doorway. He seemed to be surrounded by black smoke... 'Oh, my God, the cake!' Breaking into a run, she peered past him into the kitchen. Heather was standing beside the open oven door, wafting the smoke away with a pair of oven gloves. She was coughing theatrically.

'Oh, wow!' Simon exclaimed behind her.

'Never mind the oh, wow,' Jared said quietly. 'I have to go up to Birmingham. Will you be all right with Lian?'

'Sure. But you will be back...'

'In time for sports day, yes. I should be back tomorrow night. OK?'

Turning to Lian, he asked even more quietly, 'Will that be all right? Or were you intending to leave before then?'

Staring at him, knowing that she had no choice, she shook her head. And if he wasn't going to be there... 'Not before then, no,' she denied. Still searching his face, she wondered if he had really been asking whether he could *trust* her to look after Simon.

With a little nod, he added without even a trace of humour, or a lurking twinkle in his dark eyes, 'I think the cake got burnt.'

More ambiguity? Or a simple statement of fact? If he didn't trust her, believe in her honesty, then whatever affection he might have felt for her was presumably now dead. 'Yes,' she agreed unhappily, 'I rather think it did.'

His sigh seemed heartfelt. 'I'll go and pack an overnight bag, and then I'll be off.'

'Do you want anything to eat before you go?' she asked.

'No, thank you, I'll get something at the airport. Heather? You'd better get along to your hotel and get your own things together. I'll pick you up in about an hour.' Without another word he walked out and they heard him go upstairs. Simon went back to the barn, and Lian stared at Heather, before moving to take the ruined cake out of the oven.

'Did you ask the operator to check the line last week?' she asked quietly.

'No,' Heather denied with no trace of embarrassment.

'You just wanted me to look bad in Jared's eyes?'

'Of course.'

'And you deliberately gave Mary the wrong time for Jared to be picked up, didn't you?'

'Yes.'

Yes, something else she had glossed over, giving Heather the benefit of the doubt. Fool. 'And of course it was you who spoke to Brian Haig.'

'Yes.'

'Yet you couldn't possibly have known that I would answer the phone at that precisely convenient moment.'

Giving her a look of derision, Heather said, 'Of course I could. As soon as Jared went out for his walk, I telephoned the engineer and asked him to check the line back.'

'That devious? Just to get me into trouble?'

'To get you sent packing,' Heather qualified, 'yes, of course.'

'You don't even look *ashamed*!' Lian exclaimed helplessly.

'Ashamed? Why should I look ashamed? You get nothing in this world if you don't engineer it. And, if you think Jared will believe you if you tell him all this, he won't,' she added smugly.

'No, I know he won't.'

With a nasty little smile, Heather turned on her heel and walked out.

Were there really so many awful people in the world? People who would cheat and lie? She couldn't even comfort herself by saying that Heather was an exception, because sadly she wasn't. With a regretful look at the cake, she emptied it into the bin. And if she tried to fight Heather with the same weapons that would make her no better than the secretary. And why bother anyway? Jared didn't want her.

Everything seemed an anticlimax after that. The house was very empty without him. Even Simon was quiet, and she felt as though she'd lost something really rather precious.

He didn't get back the next night. He rang and spoke with his son, and promised to be home in time for the sports. Replacing the receiver, Simon kicked moodily at the rug. 'I bet he doesn't. I bet he's with *her*.'

'Who?' she asked gently. 'Heather?'

'Yeah. He's always with her.'

'Only at the moment; when his business is finished he'll be able to spend more time with you.'

Raising unhappy eyes to her, Simon blurted out, 'Are you really going to go?'

'Oh, Simon!' she exclaimed helplessly. With a comforting arm round his shoulders, she steered him into the lounge. Perching beside him on the sofa, she tried to explain. 'I don't really belong here, you know. I only came for a little while.'

'But you like it here! You like Dad! You were kissing him and everything! And I thought . . .'

'Thought what? That I would stay?'

'Yes! I like you! It's been really neat since you've been here!'

'What? Burnt cakes? Bad meals?' she teased, trying, she supposed, to jolly him out of it.

'Those things don't matter! They don't! Oh, Lian, don't go! Please don't!'

'Oh, Simon.' Pulling him against her, Lian leaned back. He usually acted so grown-up that she tended to forget that he was only a little boy. 'I like your father, and you, too much, I sometimes think, and the longer I stay, the harder it will be for me to eventually go. But go, I must.' With a long sigh, she stared at the opposite wall. She still felt a great deal of attraction for Jared, maybe it was even love, she didn't really know, but whatever it was his recent behaviour hadn't changed that; but she *was* disappointed in him, disappointed that he wasn't the man she had thought him.

Which made not one iota of difference to the eventual outcome, she thought drearily, because he didn't want her. But she couldn't tell his son that, so she said instead, 'You know when we were sitting on the stairs? And I told you about how I felt? Well, the feelings didn't go away, not altogether, and until they do, until I find out what I want to do with my life, I can't settle. Do you understand?'

'Does that mean you'll come back one day?' he asked hopefully.

'I don't know. It's hard to explain, but, like the way you seem to need to get into mischief, well, I need the sea. Need to be near it.' Absently stroking his hair, feeling guilty for lying to him, but seeing no other way out of a situation that was fast becoming unbearable, she added, 'It doesn't mean we can't remain friends. We can write to each other, maybe even visit.'

'But you won't be *here*!'

'No, I won't be here.' Easing him away, she smiled into Simon's woebegone face. 'On the other hand, I haven't left yet either. I shall be here for a little bit longer.'

'A month?'

'No,' she denied regretfully, 'not that long.' Only until after your father gets back, until after the sports, but she couldn't tell him that either—not now, not when he was feeling hurt and abandoned. 'Come on, cheer up, I'll give you a game of Scrabble.'

As though he too was making a determined effort, Simon said, 'Nah. You always win. Backgammon?'

'All right, backgammon it is. I baggy red.'

Jared didn't get back for sports day. He rang just before she left for the school.

'I'm stuck halfway down the bloody railway line,' he exclaimed angrily. 'There were no flights out of Birmingham, due to some bloody militant baggage-handlers' strike! No helicopters . . .'

'Helicopter?' she queried weakly as though she'd never heard of such a thing.

'Yes! Helicopter! So, fine, I thought, I'll get the train, which I stupidly assumed would be just as quick as going to Manchester and getting a flight from there. And where am I now? In a bloody siding because some vandal has ripped up the track! And we are now waiting for some half-witted body to come and mend the bloody thing! Or replace it! Or—oh, sh——'

The line went dead. Replacing the receiver, glancing at her watch to see that she had only twenty minutes before the first race started, Lian tapped her fingers impatiently on the table-top, then snatched up the receiver when it rang. 'We got cut off,' he muttered grumpily.

'But if you're stuck in a siding,' she began in puzzlement, 'how did you find a phone?'

'What?' he asked impatiently. 'It's a mobile. I borrowed it off someone.' With a long sigh, he asked more quietly, 'Will you tell Simon? Explain?'

'Yes, of course.'

'And if I'm lucky, if they do something soon, I may even make it before the finish, although that's probably the thought being father to the wish, or whatever the damned expression is. You will explain, won't you? That it wasn't deliberate?'

'Yes, of course, don't worry...' But she was holding a dead line. Replacing the receiver, she picked up her bag and started out for the school. Poor Simon. Poor Jared. Having money didn't always mean you could do what you wanted to do when you wanted to do it.

She got there just in time to see Simon trail in last in the sack race. She could see by his face that he hadn't been trying, and her heart ached for him. When he spotted her, he searched frantically round for a sign of his father. 'Dad?' he mouthed, and she reluctantly shook her head. With a look of bitter disappointment, and anger, he dodged away and went back to sit with his class before she could get across to speak to him.

He didn't try in the obstacle race either, just mucked about to make his friends laugh. She saw a teacher bend to speak to him when it was finished, saw his pretended indifference, and, unable to bear it any longer, she ducked under the rope that kept the parents off the course, and walked across to him. Grabbing his arm as he went to run back to his place, she bent to face him. 'I'm sorry I was late, but I was talking to your father on the phone. He couldn't get a flight back, so he caught the train, and someone pulled the track up...'

'Oh, sure,' he said bitterly.

'Yes, they did,' she argued firmly. 'I know it sounds ridiculous, but it's true. Your father doesn't lie, and he wanted to be here just as much as you wanted him to be. You know that. Don't you? *Don't* you?' she insisted.

He didn't answer, just glared at her, but his chin was clamped very firmly, she saw, his teeth clenched.

'And *I* came,' she said gently, 'and I do not expect my chum to come in last,' she teased. Making a fist, she touched it lightly to his chin. 'These things happen, Simon. It's no one's fault, just part of growing up, I'm afraid. So win the next race for yourself, hm? Just to show them you can.'

Lowering his eyes, he just stood there, and, knowing she could do no more, Lian gave him a hug and released him. Without looking at her, he walked back to his friends.

Poor little sausage. With a sigh, she returned to the other side of the rope barrier.

'Is he not very well?' a woman asked her.

'What? Oh, yes, he's fine, just disappointed. His father got held up and couldn't get here in time.'

'Oh.' Is that all? her tone seemed to say, and with an irritated glance Lian moved away.

Simon came second to last in the running race, then dashed off to get changed before Lian could tell him that she would wait for him by the refreshment stand. So she stood, in the hot sun, watching the door he had gone in by. She waited half an hour, which was stupid, because how many small boys took half an hour to get changed? Unless they were larking about, of course. With an irritated shake of her head, she pushed the door wide and peered in. A long corridor confronted her.

'Can I help you?'

Swinging round, she smiled in relief on recognising one of the teachers. 'I was looking for Simon Lowe. He came in about half an hour ago.'

'Hang on, then, I'll go and check.' Disappearing inside, he returned five minutes later, shaking his head. 'He apparently left ages ago with Peter Young.'

'Oh, right, thank you.' With a lame smile, she walked round the side of the school and back towards the house by way of the road. Little monkey.

His PE kit was dumped on the kitchen table, so she knew that he'd been home, but of Simon there was no sign. Enough's enough, Simon, you've made your protest. Walking out into the garden, she shaded her eyes and stared down towards the woods. Maybe he was in the barn. Cutting across the grass, she opened the barn door. No Simon. But the embryo tree-house structure was gone. So, where next? The woods? That seemed the likeliest bet. Or leave him alone to sulk?

No, she decided, that wouldn't do. Looking down at her cream skirt, which she had put on for the sports, she debated whether to go and change. It was hardly suitable for clambering about in the woods. On the other hand, enough time had been wasted already. With a mental shrug, she set off in the direction of the woods. Slipping off her sandals, she carefully waded the stream. Bending down to replace them, she heard a shout. Listening intently, she stared downstream towards the river. There were one or two trees that way, not as many as in the woods, but that was where the shout seemed to have come from, and then she heard another one, and she felt suddenly sick, because it was a child's voice, and it sounded frightened. Not bothering with her sandals, she hitched her skirt up and ran.

Not a tree-house. Of course not a tree-house. A raft. Oh, Lian, you fool. Taking it all in in one glance, the rope stretched taut between the tree and the raft, the rapidly sinking and disintegrating raft, the two small boys clinging on for dear life, she ran faster. Grabbing the rope, she yelled, 'Hang on tight; I'll try and pull it to the bank!' Bracing her feet, she began to ease the waterlogged structure towards her. She dared not pull too fast in case it came apart entirely. And then the damned thing snagged. Oh, God.

Peter looked frozen with terror as he gripped a piece of wood that was slowly, oh, so slowly parting company with the rest. Simon had one hand on the wood, one clamped into Peter's shirt. 'He can't swim!' he shouted.

And neither can I, she thought defeatedly. Then you'd better learn bloody fast, Lian! Hitching her straight skirt up as far as it would go, to give her more manoeuvrability, she slid down the bank and, with one hand on the rope for balance, waded out as far as she could without going entirely under. Her outstretched arm was nowhere near long enough to reach them. And then, to her everlasting and heartfelt relief, she saw Jared pounding along the opposite bank. He kicked off his shoes and plunged into the pond. Grabbing both boys, he thrust Peter at her, then towed

Simon to the edge, boosted him to safety, and began to haul himself out.

One hand holding the rope, the other Peter, who was clamped to her like a terrified limpet, Lian awkwardly turned and began to pull them back towards safety. The shelving bottom meant both their weights were taken by her arm, and as she pulled herself out, and tried to hoist Peter on to firm ground, she felt something tear in her back. Excruciating pain shot up her spine, and she gasped, and froze. She was barely aware of Jared taking Peter, barely aware of anything but the pain.

'You bitch!' Jared shouted. 'Oh, you bitch.' He sounded anguished. 'I trusted you!' Grabbing up both boys, he strode off, leaving her still waist-deep in the stagnant water.

Whimpering with pain, terrified that she'd done irreparable damage, she slowly dragged herself out. Using the rope, she finally made it to the tree, then just hung on as wave after wave of agony lanced up to her neck and down to her ankles. Her breathing ragged, she prayed for the pain to pass.

She didn't know how long she stood there, arms clasped round the tree, her face against the bark, only that it seemed an eternity, and she knew that she must move, get back to the house, get help. Opening her eyes, feeling sick and ill, she stared along the bank. She felt divorced from reality, and yet was aware, with almost startling clarity, of the sun, warm on her back, of the birdsong, of each leaf on each tree stirring in the gentle breeze, and she didn't want to move, didn't want to even try to walk. Wanted only to do it in her mind. But if she could get to that clump of weeds, that next tree ...

Cautiously loosening her grip, she took a step, and screamed. Oh, dear God. Whimpering once more, she bent slightly, and found it easier, not much, but easier, and if she didn't actually lift her foot, just slid it along the ground, she thought she might be able to manage.

With a sort of limping shuffle, she made it to the clump of weeds, to the tree, and the next, and the next, not thinking, just blanking her mind to everything but the need to move. She passed her abandoned sandals, used Simon's Tarzan rope to support herself across the stream, managed, somehow, to get up the far bank. And all the time, on the long, painful journey, she kept a picture of the house in her mind— of her room, of the bed she would lie on, and slowly, excruciatingly slowly, she got to the kitchen, the hall, used the banisters to hoist herself upwards.

She found she had to consciously tell herself things in order to do them. Bedside cabinet, pain-killers she'd been given before. Bathroom, swallow pills, put in plug, run hot water, take off clothes. With a last effort, she climbed into the bath, eased herself backwards, closed her eyes in relief, and prayed.

Please God don't let it be too bad. Please God take away the pain. Let me not be a cripple, let me not be an invalid; and as she lay there, fighting the pain, waiting for the pain-killers to work, trying to relax her muscles, not cramp them tight, she was aware of voices, of Jared's deep tones, of Simon's tearful ones.

'You didn't come!' Simon shouted.

'Is that any reason to try to kill yourself?' Jared demanded furiously. 'I asked Lian to explain, didn't she?'

'No!'

Oh, Simon, she thought weakly. She knew he was only saying it in fear and temper, because he was hurt and bewildered, but she doubted that Jared in his present temper would. Tuning their voices out as a wave of sickness washed over her, she took deep, slow breaths to try to combat it. Perhaps she shouldn't have had the water so hot; perhaps she should have taken only two pain-killers instead of four.

Feeling dreadfully ill, she groped behind her to pull out the plug, then slowly got herself to her knees, to her feet, and climbed out. Sitting on the edge of the bath, her head bowed, she waited for a wave of pain to pass, before dragging the towel towards her and roughly drying herself. One hand on the basin, she dragged herself across to the door, unhooked her robe and managed somehow to get into it. Opening the bathroom door, she leaned weakly against the jamb and stared at the bed. Such an impossibly long way away—then jumped when the bedroom door crashed open and Jared strode in.

'Why?' he demanded savagely. 'Pique? Or a complete lack of care and compassion? Because your own damned selfish troubles took precedence over anyone else's? They're children!' he yelled as he strode across to her. 'Nine years old! And you deliberately endangered their lives! Why? Because you couldn't take part in a race of your own? You nearly drowned my son!' he shouted. 'You even helped him make the bloody raft!'

Staring at him, feeling clammy and ill, Lian barely heard him, barely registered his words, and it wasn't until he grabbed the lapel of her robe in one bunched fist and shook her that she made any sound at all. A whimper.

'You couldn't even be bothered to tell him why I couldn't get to the sports, could you? I asked you and asked you to explain——' Breaking off, he stared at her, and only then seemed to become aware of the state she was in. 'What's wrong?' he demanded, no less aggressively, but almost as though he thought it a ploy to gain sympathy. And when she didn't answer he asked more hesitantly, 'Lian?'

Incapable of speech, she made a blind, groping gesture towards the bed, then whimpered and shrank back as he made a move as if to lift her.

'Oh, God.' Grasping her shoulders to steady her, he supported her and let her take her own shuffling pace towards the bed. Held her as she cautiously lowered herself, then lay back. Closing her eyes, she gave a shuddering little sigh. 'Dr Gregory,' she whispered raggedly, 'Portsmouth Hospital. Tell him—back gone.'

She vaguely heard him leave, heard him thunder down the stairs, heard the ping as he lifted the phone, and then everything became a pain-filled blur. She was distantly aware of someone demanding to know how many pills she'd taken, and managed to tell them. Only half aware of being lifted on to a stretcher and carried out, she had a distant recollection of noise, shuddering movement, and then nothing until she woke in a hospital bed and found Dr Gregory leaning over her.

'Not very clever, Miss Grayson,' he reproved pleasantly. 'However, we've X-rayed you, found the trouble, and, in about two hours, I'm going to operate. All right?'

'Yes,' she whispered.

With a smile, he added, 'You're lucky to have such wealthy friends. National Health would have taken a bit longer. You haven't the faintest idea what I'm talking about, have you?'

'No.'

'Jared Lowe hired a helicopter to bring you here. Hired this private room, hired my services, and all without having to step outside his own house,' he said admiringly.

'He isn't here?'

'Here? No. Should he have been?'

'No,' she agreed emptily.

'So, two hours instant enough for you?'

'Yes. What did I do to it?'

'In layman's terms you displaced—well, for want of a better word—the disc you damaged before. It's pressing on several nerves, hence the pain. There is some small risk involved in the operation—there always is of course when mucking about near the spinal cord—but I have performed it many times before,' he added with a grin, 'with, I might add, a hundred per cent success-rate.'

'And if I don't have it?'

'You will be in constant pain, my dear.'

'And when it's done will it be better? As strong as it was before?'

'For emulating Hornblower? No,' he denied gently. 'For normal everyday behaviour it will be fine, but I would have to advise against strenuous activity. You will, hopefully, be able to dance, jump, run. But weight-lifting? No.'

'I see.' Giving Dr Gregory a wan smile, Lian obediently signed the permission form. 'Thank you.'

'You'll have to be a famous something else instead,' he said kindly. 'Writer? Photographer? You've got a brain, Lian, try using that instead of muscle. Hm? Nurse will be along soon to sort you out. I'll see you later.'

When she opened her eyes the following morning it took her a moment to orientate herself, to recall all that had happened, and she felt incredibly thirsty. She was lying on her side, a cage of some sort across her, and she had a vague recollection of someone telling her that she had to lie still, not roll on to her back, and she supposed the cage was to ensure that she did as she was told. She also realised, belatedly, that the excruciating pain had gone. She hurt, felt sore, but not the agony of previously. Closing her eyes, she went back to sleep.

That first week in the hospital dragged incredibly slowly. She had no visitors, because no one knew she was there. Apart from Jared, of course. She'd had a card from Simon, her suitcase and a note from Mary wishing her well. She was bored and lonely, and self-pity rode on her shoulder, despite her constant attempts to shake it off. First David, then the accident, the loss of her beloved racing, then Jared—and all in the space of a couple of months. Not a very good track record. Was someone Up There trying to tell her something?

The nurses were kind and efficient, but they just didn't have time to spend chatting to her, so most of her days were spent watching the television. She watched extraordinary soap operas; gardening hints; cooking, and interviews with the rich and famous. She also, with a rather morbid fascination, watched the start of the round-the-world yacht race—and didn't know if she grizzled for that, or Jared, or her injury.

Two days before she was due to be discharged she had an unexpected visitor. Simon. He eased hesitantly into her room, a look of trepidation on his young face.

'Lian?' he whispered.

Staring at him, she felt tears prick her eyes. She'd missed him. With a warm smile, she held out her hand to him. 'What a lovely surprise.'

Closing the door, he hurried towards her, and she assumed that Jared still couldn't bear to see her and was waiting outside.

'I came on the train,' he announced bluntly, and somewhat belligerently.

'Did you?' And only then registered the 'I'. 'Your father isn't with you?' she asked with a frown.

'No.' His face flushed; his mouth set, he blustered, 'He wouldn't bring me, so I came on my own!'

'You did what?' she exclaimed in horror. 'Oh, Simon, he'll be going out of his mind.'

'I don't care! He said you were hurt and he wouldn't bring me!'

'But how on earth did you find the way?'

'On the map,' he said proudly. 'I knew the address, because of the card I sent, and Mary helped me find it on the map.'

'She knew you were coming?'

'No!' he denied scornfully. 'I just told her I wanted to know where it was.'

'Oh, Simon,' Lian said again helplessly. 'It's lovely to see you, and it was very kind of you to come, but we really must let your father know. Let me get the nurse to ring him and let him know you're—safe,' she concluded lamely as the door burst open to admit a very grim-looking Jared. Taking in his white face, the frantic expression in his eyes, she reached for Simon's hand and gave it a gentle squeeze.

Staring at his son, as though he couldn't yet quite believe that he was safe, he slumped back against the door and let all his breath out in relief.

'You should have let me come!' Simon shouted defiantly.

'Yes,' Jared agreed quietly. 'I'm sorry. I was angry.'

'I came on the train,' Simon whispered, his eyes fixed widely on his father. 'I had to change.'

'Oh, Simon.' Holding out his arms, Jared gripped the boy hard when the boy hurled himself into them. When he'd mastered himself to some degree, he looked across at Lian. 'How are you?' he asked flatly, yet his look clearly accused her of causing more trouble between himself and his son.

'All right.'

With a little nod, he partially released Simon. 'I'll wait for you outside.'

'You don't want to stay?' Simon pleaded.

'No, I don't want to stay.'

Opening the door, he walked out and Simon worriedly trailed back to the bed. 'Why is he angry with you, Lian?'

'Oh, because it was my fault you made the raft.'

'But it wasn't,' he denied.

'Yes, it was. I should have known it wasn't for a tree-house. And then, when it all fell apart, I couldn't save you. If your father hadn't come along——' Breaking off, she swallowed hard, because if Jared hadn't come along they would probably both have drowned, and that was the stuff of nightmares.

'It would have been all right,' he said, not very confidently. 'You'd have come in for us.'

'No,' she whispered. 'I can't swim, you see.'

'You can't?'

'No.' Deliberately forcing the images away, she said more brightly, 'Never mind all that now; tell me what you've been up to.' For the next half-hour he regaled her with tales of the trips he had made with his father. 'And we went to London, and Dad took me out in a rowing-boat on the lake in the big park.'

'Did he?'

'Yeah. He wasn't very good. We kept going round in circles,' he laughed, then sobered. 'But I wish you'd been there.'

'Yes, I wish I had too.' Stretching out her hand, she pushed his tumbled hair back off his forehead. Hair like his father's. With a little sigh, and a faint smile, she said, 'You'd best not stay too long; your father will be getting fed up, waiting by himself outside.'

'Yeah,' Simon agreed despondently. 'Can I come again?'

'Not on your own. Promise?'

Nodding, he suddenly darted forward and kissed her awkwardly on the cheek. His face flushed, as though he was embarrassed, then he hurried out and quietly closed the door.

Unbearably touched, Lian lay back tiredly, and let her tears overflow. Yet the image that remained in her mind wasn't of Simon, but of his father. How he had looked, what he had worn—and the expression on his face. And now you must put it all behind you, Lian, get on with your life, she told herself. Reaching out her hand, she rang for the nurse, then asked for the telephone to be wheeled in. She would ring her father, tell him what had happened, ask if she could go and stay for a while.

'How will you get down?' he asked worriedly.

'On the train...'

'You will not! I'll come and pick you up.'

In the event, he didn't need to. He rang her that evening to explain that Jem Trewson had to come into Southampton the next day and had offered to do a detour and pick her up. Getting permission to be released a day early, she was wheeled down to Reception to wait for him. Jem wasn't a man for conversation, which suited her, and the journey was completed in virtual silence.

They arrived at her father's cottage just as the evening sun was beginning its slow descent. The hill, with its scattering of quaint houses, lay behind them, the sea in front. The wistaria-covered walls were a riot of colour, the gate freshly painted, and a shimmer of tears filled her eyes. It was her father's way of saying welcome. Every time, in all the years since they had moved here, whenever she was expected home, the gate was given a fresh coat of paint. Asking Jem to leave her case by the gate, she thanked him and climbed out. Walking the few yards to the edge of the cliff, she stared out over the sea, took a deep breath of the fresh, tangy air, and gave a long sigh almost of contentment. To taste the salt on her tongue, feel the wind in her hair, hear the cry of the gulls meant that she was home.

Hearing a sound behind her, the opening of the cottage door, she turned and walked carefully towards the tall, grey-haired man with the tanned, weather-beaten face, and her own grey eyes. They stood, one either side of the newly painted gate, and smiled at each other. Then Nick Grayson unlatched the barrier, and took his daughter in his arms.

'Welcome home, darling.'

'Thanks,' she said huskily.

After their meal, and having explained, honestly, all that had happened since her father had last seen her, Lian went for a short solitary walk up to the headland. Not too far, just far enough to try to get things into perspective, come to terms with everything, put it behind her.

She returned via the lane at the back of the cottage, and through the back garden. Walking into the lounge, she halted in shock. Jared was lying back in one of the chintz-covered easy-chairs. 'Hello, Lian,' he greeted quietly as he got to his feet.

She had just spent ages telling herself that it was over, that she would never see him again, and here he was. It seemed almost too much to bear. 'What are you doing here?' she asked despairingly.

'Looking for you. Your father has taken Simon out, down to the harbour, I think.'

'Oh,' she murmured lamely. 'How is he?'

'Chastened. Why can't you swim?'

'What?' she asked blankly.

'On the way back from the hospital Simon and I had a long talk—should you be standing?' he asked with a frown of concern. 'Here, come and sit down.' Arranging the cushion at one end of the settee, he guided her across to it as though she were an invalid.

Easing herself down, moving the cushion into a more comfortable position, Lian continued to just stare at him. 'A long talk?' she prompted helplessly.

'Yes.' Perching beside her, he leaned forward, arms along his thighs, a position that flooded her mind with memories of another day, another time. 'He explained about the safe, the raft, sports day. I went way over the top, didn't I?' Picking up her hand, which lay curled loosely on her lap, he stared down at it. Absently playing with her fingers, he explained quietly, 'I think that last week will have to go down in history as the biggest cock-up of all time. Everything that could go wrong did. Files going missing, documents, odd phone calls...'

'I truly didn't take that call,' she insisted quietly.

Lifting his head, he searched her eyes. 'No. My beloved Miss Gentle told me a few home-truths about Heather, about little lies she'd been caught out in, her eye to the main chance.'

'Like you?'

'So it would seem. According to my Miss Gentle, anyway. When she asked me what the devil was the matter with me, in anger and frustration, it all came spilling out: the phone calls, the raft, the lot. And she told me I was a fool. She met you once, and knew you for what you were.' With a faint smile he asked, 'Do you remember what she said to you?'

'That I would do,' she murmured.

'Yes. For me, she meant.'

'For you?' she echoed weakly.

'Yes.'

But he didn't want her for him. 'And Heather?' she asked.

'Has been sacked. I'm sorry,' he apologised contritely.

'It's all right. Understandable, really, that you should take her part, and I have to admit, the tale of the telephone engineer sounded a bit implausible.'

'Yes,' he agreed with a faint smile.

'And before that you'd found me, as you thought, rifling your safe.'

'Yes.'

'Just who exactly is Brian Haig?' she asked curiously, and in an effort to deflect the conversation from the personal.

'One of Lowe's biggest customers. I'd spent ages trying to persuade him not to take his business elsewhere, and just when I thought I'd succeeded he rang...'

'And so you had to go up to Birmingham.'

'Mm. And oh, Lian, you wouldn't believe the nightmare of trying to get back. All I wanted was to finish with the whole damned mess, get back to Simon, see his sports, get my life back on an even keel. I was angry and disappointed that you had turned out to be a liar, furious when Haig couldn't see me the evening we arrived; then, when we'd eventually had the meeting, there were no damned flights out of Birmingham. Someone dug the track up...

'I felt so helpless and frustrated—not a feeling I enjoy. I practically hijacked someone's mobile phone, shouted at you, and then eventually rang my beloved Miss Gentle—who really deserves a massive rise— dragged her from her sick-bed, and insisted, probably savagely, that she find me a helicopter and get it to me stat!

'Bless her, she did, and I arrived in time to see, as I thought, you pulling the raft across the pond in direct contradiction to my orders that Simon was not to go in a raft race. And then, as I ran furiously along the bank to give you hell, saw, to my horror, that it was disintegrating; saw Peter almost under the water, saw Simon trying to hold him up, and you dithering about on the opposite bank, your skirt above your knees, not even attempting to get into the water to save them . . .'

'Because I couldn't swim,' she put in unhappily. 'Dear God, do you think I don't know how you must have been feeling about that? I have nightmares about it! If you hadn't come . . . I keep telling myself that I would have plunged in, of course I would—but would I?'

'But *why* can't you swim?' he exclaimed in astonishment. 'You're a sailor, for goodness' sake!'

With a faint smile, she said, 'I don't personally know any sailors who can swim. There must be some, but I don't know of any.'

'But don't the race rules say you must?'

'No. Nor that you have to wear a safety-line. Daft, isn't it?'

'But that's crazy!'

'Not really,' she denied. 'If you fall overboard out at sea, the chances of being found again are minimal, unless it's fantastically calm, which is rare. And in the middle of the ocean where would you swim to? You'll drown eventually, so why prolong the agony? If you can swim, it's an automatic reaction to at least try. And to what purpose? It's better to drown quickly, get it over with. Don't look so horrified; accidents are pretty rare.'

'Are they?' he queried, and something in his face stopped her insisting. 'My wife couldn't swim,' he told her almost inaudibly.

'And she drowned?' she whispered in horror.

'Yes. In a yachting accident. And when I saw Simon struggling in the water—I thought I was going to lose him too.'

'Oh, Jared. So that's why you wouldn't let him go in the raft race. Even though he could swim.'

'Yes. Perhaps it was stupid, perhaps I was being over-protective, but I couldn't bear to lose him. And then I stormed off and left you in pain,' he continued, perhaps in a determined effort to dispel other, more horrifying mental pictures. 'How in God's name did you ever get back to the house?'

'With a great deal of difficulty,' she confessed almost inaudibly. Then, actually remembering that nightmare journey, she gave a little shudder. 'I don't even want to think about it! But you can't blame me more than I blame myself. I should have known it wasn't for a tree-house.'

'Perhaps, but it doesn't excuse my jumping to conclusions. About anything. Although why the hell you couldn't have explained . . . about the safe, about the raft . . .'

'Because I never explain,' Lian told him with a wan smile. 'And because I was finding it hard right then coming to terms with the fact that I was no longer in charge of my life. I've always been the director, not the directed, and I rather resented being treated as though I were the same age as Simon. And I've never been very good at being told what to do,' she added.

None of it was really true, but it sounded plausible, didn't it? Sounded better than telling him that being blamed really didn't matter that much—because his not loving her mattered so much more.

'No, you're very capable and sure of yourself, aren't you?' he queried with what looked like a forced grin. 'You sat there in my study that first day as though there were a very nasty smell under your nose, and you looked at me as though I was the most useless thing in creation—and I was very, very intrigued.'

'And then proceeded to browbeat me into staying.'

'Mm.'

'I wonder what would have happened if I'd liked Mrs Popplewell?' she murmured. She was finding it very hard to concentrate, to keep her attention on their conversation.

'Oh, I think I might have spiked a few guns.' Releasing her hand, Jared gently trailed his fingers down her cheek. 'So I'm sorry, Lian. I've behaved abominably to you, haven't I? And to Simon.'

Suppressing the shiver that his touch caused, she lowered her eyes, afraid that he might see in them her desire to turn her mouth into his palm, lean against his strong shoulder. 'How else were you to behave,' she asked huskily, 'believing me to be untrustworthy?'

'The right thing for all the wrong reasons,' he commented. 'And then to find he'd disappeared. Dear lord, Lian, but I was frightened.'

'Yes,' she agreed inadequately. 'Something else to blame me for.'

'And why in heaven's name did I never suspect that he could do it?' he demanded, not picking her up on the accusation. 'And change trains! You have to admit that he's resourceful.'

'Yes, he's certainly that. And kind. He sent me a card, did you know?'

'Yes,' Jared agreed quietly. 'He has more sense than his father.'

Not wishing to dwell on that, Lian asked hastily, 'Where did he get the money for the fare?'

'Emptied his money-box.' With a long sigh, he got to his feet. 'Well, I'd better be going. I still have to find somewhere to stay for the night.'

'Yes.'

He seemed constrained now, as though he no longer knew what to say. But then, neither did she, and it was almost a relief when she heard the front door open, and Simon and her father's voices as they came in.

'Right, well, I'd best be off.'

'Yes.'

Turning abruptly, Jared walked into the hall, presumably to intercept his son.

CHAPTER SIX

'YOU'LL find it hard to get rooms this time of year!'
Lian heard her father exclaim. 'It's the height of the
holiday season!'

She heard Jared's deep voice in reply, but not the
words, and then her father again, and she closed her
eyes in despair.

'Why not stay here? We've plenty of room. Glad
to have you.'

Oh, Dad, no. He was trying to be helpful, she knew,
thought he was doing it for her—and if she hadn't
told him how she felt about Jared...

'Then that's settled,' he said in hearty satisfaction.
'Simon, go and help your dad bring your cases in.'

Cases? Lian wondered in confusion. She'd assumed they had just come down overnight. Eyeing
her father's half-hopeful, half-sheepish expression
when he joined her in the lounge, she gave him a look
of disgust. 'What on earth did you do that for? And
how long are they staying?' she hissed.

'Not pleased, darling?' he queried hesitantly. 'He
likes you...'

'Oh, Dad!'

'He does, and now that you've got the misunderstandings sorted out—you have, haven't you?'

'Yes,' she admitted. 'But it doesn't make any
difference.'

'It might.'

'The eternal optimist——' she murmured. Hearing Simon and his father return, she broke off and looked away. It wouldn't work, it couldn't. It would just get embarrassing. 'I'd better go and make up some beds.'

'I'll do it,' her father offered hastily.

Leaning back, she pulled a face. She didn't want this... Well, she did, of course she did, but you couldn't make someone care for you if they didn't, could you? If he had cared for her he wouldn't have made that joke about Miss Gentle thinking her right for him.

'Do you mind so very much, Lian?' Jared asked quietly from the doorway.

Looking up with a start, she shook her head. 'No, of course not,' she mumbled. What else could she say? It was the obvious solution. 'I just assumed that you were only down overnight.'

'No. Simon has six weeks' summer holiday,' he explained slowly as he walked further into the room. 'The management team in the London office are beginning to trickle back, Miss Gentle should be recovered next week, so I've decided to take a long holiday. We decided, *both* of us,' he emphasised, 'that we would like to be near the sea. And it seemed a good idea to kill two birds with one stone, so to speak. Make our peace with you——' Breaking off when his son erupted into the room behind him, he turned to smile at him. 'All right, all settled in?'

'Yeah. It's really great. Hi, Lian,' he added with a little of the constraint that his father was using.

'Hi yourself.'

'Is it all right?' he asked awkwardly of no one in particular.

'Sure,' Lian insisted. 'Really neat.'

With a hesitant grin, which widened when Lian gave one of her own, he looked at his father. 'Nick said I...'

'Nick?' his father queried pointedly.

'Yeah, Lian's dad—he said I could call him Nick, and he said there are lots of things to do down here. There's a model railway, a model village, boats, bays, lots!'

'Then you'd best go and get some sleep in order to be ready for all these adventures, hadn't you?'

'Oh-h,' he began to protest.

'Scat, it's gone ten.'

'OK,' he capitulated. ''Night, Dad, night, Lian.'

''Night,' they echoed.

Alone with Jared once more, Lian looked down and fiddled aimlessly with her watch. 'Is it what you want?' she finally asked. 'To stay here?'

'Yes.'

Glancing up, she flushed when she saw the warmth in his eyes. 'I don't want...'

'Anything more?' he finished for her.

Puzzled, she opened her mouth to query it, when he went on, 'Then can we just be friends?' he asked softly. 'As we once were? Relax and enjoy ourselves? It's been a long time since I had a holiday by the sea.'

With a reluctant smile, she teased, 'Mm, I can imagine. Not your scene somehow.'

'No,' he agreed just as softly. 'However...'

Then why do it? she wondered. Only for Simon's sake? Because his son liked her?

The next two weeks didn't really help clarify her thoughts. Jared treated her rather as if she were his sister. Or Simon's sister, and yet, just sometimes,

didn't tension spring between them? Didn't he sometimes seem about to say something? Or was that only
wishful thinking? And yet even being just friends was
better than nothing. Or was it? Might it truly not have
been better never to see him again?

Physically she was better; the weeks of sun, of pottering about, taking things easily had brought her back
to full health. And if there was a constant yearning
for things that were probably unobtainable, then she
mostly tried to bury them very firmly. With a sigh,
wishing futilely that she could stop wanting more than
she could ever have, she lay back on the warm sand.
To make matters worse, Jared, Simon and her father
got on like a house on fire, seemed to find endless
things to talk about. Both Jared and his son were more
relaxed, happy, and, for a millionaire, he seemed to
have taken to the simple life with a vengeance. A
rather bitter-sweet light in her eyes, Lian tried to make
herself believe that she was content just to be friends
with him, regain her strength, only it was a lie.

They were all out at the moment with old Sam
Taylor in his fishing-boat, had been since dawn, and
not expected back until around four o'clock. Her
family, or so she sometimes foolishly pretended.
Father, husband and son. A sad smile on her mouth,
she daydreamed of how it might have been, had he
loved her. The yearning to sail was still there, of
course—maybe it always would be—but it was not
such a powerful need as before. Not so driving—and
not so necessary to her happiness as Jared and his
son.

Perhaps she would cook them a meal when they got
back; that would give them a shock, change the
rhythm. Walk with Jared on the headland maybe...

Fool. Needing to distract her thoughts, she got lithely to her feet. There was only a small twinge in her back to remind her of her injury as she pulled on her shorts and T-shirt and made her way back to the house. The doctor had said two weeks before she should resume a more normal lifestyle, and the two weeks were now up, thank goodness.

Five o'clock came and went. Six, and by half-past she had passed worry, anxiety, anger, and was now quite convinced that something had happened. That there had been an accident. Could even see, with vivid clarity, the explosion on board, the four bodies hurled into the sea. Visualise their struggles for survival ... No! Yet didn't she, of all people, know what a hard taskmaster the sea could be? How fickle? How cruel? And because she could no longer challenge it, conquer it, had it taken the three people she loved best in the world?

And she did love them, all of them, desperately— and now it was too late. Stop it! Just stop right there. They'll be fine. They'll come waltzing in that door any minute now, laughing, joking, no thought for anything but the great day they'd had. Well, how dared they put her through all this worry? How dared they?

With jerky, uncoordinated movements, she straightened the place-mats, rearranged the knives and forks, and knew that if she hadn't prepared a meal they'd have been home on time. If she'd just lazed on the beach, none of this would have happened. With an impatient gesture, she flung down one of the napkins—napkins, for God's sake!—and stormed out to the front door. Striding down the path, she leaned on the gate and stared down towards the quay. Any minute now!

Seven o'clock, eight. She'd been down to the quay, up to the headland, back to the quay. She'd rung the coastguard, and then hung up before he could answer, and was just about to try him again when she heard them. Laughing. Slamming down the receiver, she practically flew along the hall, and all the hours spent in fear and anguish exploded in fury. Wrenching open the front door, she glared at the three figures just coming up the path. They were chatting and laughing as though nothing had happened.

'You look ni——' Jared began, then closed his mouth in comical surprise when she launched into the attack.

'Where the hell have you been?' she demanded. 'I've been going out of my mind! Four, you said! Four! It is now gone eight!'

'We——' her father began, only to be interrupted.

'I've been worried sick! Sick!' Lian repeated as though it was necessary to repeat herself in order to emphasise the importance of it. 'But do you care? No! You come strolling in here as though time doesn't exist! As though you're the only people in the world who matter! Selfish! Just like all men! Selfish to the core! Well, that's it! That is bloody it! I'm not doing anything for any of you ever again! Ever!' Whirling back into the house, she launched herself upstairs and into her room, locked the door, and threw herself across the bed, where she indulged in a healthy bout of crying.

'Whoops,' her father said.

Smothering their guilt with sniggers, they crept into the house. Sobered when they saw the beautifully set

table, investigated the kitchen and found the salad
tossed, the wine opened, the steaks ready under the
grill.

Her throat and chest aching from the tears she had
shed, Lian rolled over on to her back and stared up
at the ceiling. All taps at the door she ignored. All
soft calls asking if she was all right. All whispered
apologies. Bastards, all of them. She also felt extremely stupid. She'd behaved like a silly girl, like a
fishwife. She also felt sick from the residual fear, cer-
tainty that she had lost them all. And she didn't want
to face them, see amusement perhaps at her outburst.
The morning would be soon enough.

The soft knock on the door early the next morning
woke her, and when it was repeated she stared at it
warily as she remembered in awful clarity her behaviour of the night before.

'Lian?' Jared called softly.

Climbing from the bed, she hurried across, unlocked the door, then dashed back to huddle beneath
the covers.

When he walked in, bearing a breakfast tray, he
gave her a tentative smile. He was still in his robe, she
saw with surprise, and, avoiding his amused glance,
she hoisted herself upright and tucked the duvet se-
curely round her.

'Not talking to me?' he asked softly.

'Yes,' she muttered, still without looking at him.

'Good. I brought your breakfast.' Balancing the
tray across her knees, he perched on the edge of the
bed. 'I'm sorry, Lian,' he apologised sincerely. 'You
were perfectly right to be so angry; we were way out
of order.'

'I was worried,' she mumbled as she stared rather fixedly at the tray.

'Yes. There are no excuses I can make, because, quite simply, we forgot the time.' Reaching out, he gently tucked a strand of hair behind her ear, then tilted her chin towards him. 'I'm sorry,' he repeated. 'We all are.'

Lifting her lashes, she stared into his eyes, then gave a faint, chagrined smile. 'I sounded like a fishwife, didn't I?'

'Mm,' he agreed, just the faintest twitch to his mouth.

'I thought you were all dead.' Sobering, she looked down as she recalled her conviction of the day before. 'Thought I'd lost you all.' Looking back at him, she added earnestly, 'Don't ever do that to me again.'

'No.'

'I couldn't cope with it. I really couldn't.'

His eyes still holding hers, Jared touched his fingers gently to her cheek, caressed the warm, soft skin. 'Couldn't you?' he asked softly.

'No.'

'Why?'

'Why?' she asked in astonishment. 'Because...'

'Because?' he prompted.

'Yes, because.' Seeing the trap opening up before her, a trap of her own stupid making, she blustered, 'Because I'm fond of you and Simon.'

'Only fond?' he persisted.

'Yes,' she muttered, refusing to meet his eyes. 'Fond.'

'Oh.'

'What do you mean, oh?' she demanded.

'Nothing,' he murmured, sounding regretful. 'Just the hope that it might be more.'

'More?'

'Mm.'

'Why?'

'Because I went and did what I promised myself I wouldn't do.'

Staring at him, a faint, excited hope beginning to stir, she whispered, 'What?'

'Don't you know? You think I get sand in my sandwiches for just anyone?'

'Damn you, Jared,' she burst out thickly, 'just what are you trying to say?'

'That I really rather think I fell in love with you. In fact I think I've been in love with you since the first day you sat in my study, all frosty-faced and angry. You aren't in the least intimidated by me, are you? Not in the least envious of my wealth?'

'No,' she denied inaudibly, wondering what the hell that had to do with anything. In love with her?

'Not once, after you found out who I was, did you change, try to impress me, flirt with me—calculate.'

'No.'

'Why? Because it didn't matter? Because I didn't matter?'

'No.'

'No?' he queried with a faint smile.

'No. People are people, and you either like them or you don't,' she muttered foolishly, and a bit confusingly. In love with her? 'Your wealth has never mattered to me.'

'But I do?' he asked quietly.

With a violent nod, quite unable, she found, to articulate any further, she almost compulsively rearranged the toast on her plate, her eyes on her task.

'Then why,' he demanded, softly and very forcefully, 'didn't you say so when I told you what Miss Gentle had said the first evening here?'

'What?'

'I said——'

'I know what you said! I thought it was a joke you were trying to share with me!'

'Good grief, and you're supposed to be an intelligent woman?'

'Well, what else was I supposed to think?' Lian demanded, incensed.

'That I was falling in love with you! Why the hell else do you think I came down here?'

'To apologise—you said so!'

Grabbing the tray, he thumped it down on the bedside table, caught her against him and kissed her hard. Then kissed her again. 'Two weeks,' he muttered. 'Two wasted weeks.'

Staring up at him, she gave a slow, happy smile. 'You said it was only a light flirtation. And then you didn't even like me any more. And I thought you were probably still in love with your wife. At first you wouldn't even talk about her...'

'Because that's usually an opening gambit,' he explained with a wry smile.

'From women?' she frowned.

'Mm. An eagerness to know what she was like, in order to copy her, I can only presume.'

'Because?'

'Because they wanted to promote my interest, because I'm wealthy...'

'Oh, come on. You have mirrors in your house! You know it's more than that!'

'Not necessarily. There is a certain type of woman— who, sadly, seem to be the only sort I ever get to meet—who only wants money. They have this rather odd, and totally inaccurate idea that money buys happiness. That jewellery, attending various functions, seeing and being seen is the answer to all life's little problems.'

'Shallow,' she murmured, still examining his delightful face. 'And after you found me poking about in your safe you thought I had become one of them, didn't you?'

'Yes,' he admitted, 'and that I think, more than anything, shames me—the fact that I could have thought it of you; but people do change, you see, when they find out about my wealth.'

'And so you were always half expecting it.'

'Yes, so it was the nicest feeling when you seemed to find me ordinary. The very nicest feeling. And if it hadn't been for an error, a case of mistaken identity, I'd never even have met you. That frightens me a bit, Lian—life's happiness depending on fate.'

'Because you like to be in control?'

'Mm. Like you,' he added softly. Settling himself more comfortably on the bed, one hand idly tracing her cheek, her neck, Jared continued quietly, huskily, 'And if you hadn't been a sailor perhaps I would have, consciously, admitted how I felt about you sooner.'

Startled, she queried, 'Sailor?'

'Yes. My wife drowned when out sailing, and I'd look at you, and tell myself, no, never again. And anyway I didn't want to marry, I was happy as I was. Simon was happy as he was. All lies, Lian. But I wasn't going to get involved with a sailor. I once told you not to fall in love with me, remember?' When she nodded, he continued, 'I think I was really telling myself not to fall in love with you.'

'Because I was a sailor,' she echoed stupidly.

'Yes, and because I thought that perhaps it would always matter more to you than I would.'

'But it doesn't,' she denied.

Both their voices had grown softer during their exchange, and now he asked almost under his breath, 'How are you feeling?'

'Almost back to normal,' she told him, her voice thick, husky. 'Hardly a twinge these last few days.'

'Good. Your father has taken Simon out. There's a model village somewhere around that he wanted to see. Which means . . .'

'That the house is empty,' she finished for him, and she was suddenly finding it very difficult to breathe. Delicious warmth was spreading through her, a shivering awareness. For the past two weeks she had tried to pretend it didn't matter, that sexual tension was a figment of her imagination, and now that she knew it wasn't she was finding it difficult to come to terms with. 'You didn't . . .'

'Say anything? Show anything?'

'No.'

'Because I had to wait to see if I was forgiven, and then I thought you wanted only friendship. And then I began to think I'd been wrong, but I had to wait until you were fit, didn't I? I didn't think just kissing and the odd cuddle would be enough. Knew it wouldn't be enough, and these last two weeks have strained my patience to the utmost limit.'

'And now I'm fit, and you're forgiven—and you know how I feel.'

'Yes. And now I want to make love to you.'

Suppressing her groan of desire, Lian asked thickly, 'Do I get to eat my breakfast first?'

'No,' he denied equally thickly as he dragged her back into his arms. His mouth was hungry, almost savage as he tipped her back against the stacked pillows, as though it had been too long, too hard to bear, not being able to hold her, kiss her. When he released her they were both breathing raggedly.

'I need to clean my teeth,' she whispered dazedly.

'Then go and do them. Quickly.'

'Come back in five minutes,' she instructed huskily.

With an abrupt movement, he rose and went out, and as soon as he had closed the door she let all her breath out on a fluttery little sigh. In love with her. He was in love with her!

Shaking like a leaf, she slipped from the bed and hurried into the bathroom. She cleaned her teeth, brushed her hair, and when he returned she was lying, artfully arranged, on top of the duvet.

With a slow, delighted smile, he removed his robe, and walked across to join her. Taking her hands, he moved them gently above her head so that she was spread-eagled.

Lowering her lashes, almost afraid that it wasn't true, that she had misunderstood, she informed him demurely, 'I'm not allowed to wrestle.'

His laugh was full of exuberance and delight, and, hugging her warm body to his, he exclaimed, 'Oh, Lian, I find you utterly adorable.'

'Well, thank goodness!' For some silly reason it seemed very important that he see her as happy and laughing and flirtatious, not desperate, which was really the case. Why? she wondered as she gave him a wide smile that only just managed to hide her nervous excitement. Because she was afraid to let him see how vulnerable he could make her? 'And I'll have you know I don't behave like this for just any old body!'

Chuckling, he rubbed his nose against hers. 'I'm very pleased to hear it, but if you can't wrestle, which let me tell you has quite ruined my whole well-thought-out campaign, we'd best think of something else to do.'

'Mm, Scrabble? Trivial Pursuit?'

'Pursuit certainly,' he approved throatily, 'but I sure as hell don't feel very trivial.'

'No. Oh, Jared, make love to me,' Lian pleaded.

With a groan, he lowered his mouth back to hers, parted it, explored the sweetness within. Curved his large, warm palms beneath her, held her to him; dragged in a deep breath of control, moved, slid downwards and his mouth roved from lip to neck, to her exquisite breasts, to her waist, her hard, flat stomach; explored the hollows of her pelvis, and she arched against him in pleasure, in desire, in need. His hands were sure, expert, his palms warm, large, competent and knowing, his mouth an exquisite instrument that sought out each zone of pleasure, took each offering willingly until Lian needed to explore him as thoroughly as he was exploring her; needed to feel his warm flesh beneath her tongue, between her teeth. With a little sound of frustration, she rolled him on to his back, moved to cover him, her hair a warm, silky curtain that enclosed them in a private world of their own. A world of touch and taste, erotic pleasure, safe from intrusion.

Their movements surer, more intense, greedy, savage almost, he pulled her up to straddle him, held her, his hands heavy on her thighs, arched to meet her; needed more, needed to be in control, pulled her down to him, her breasts just brushing his, then crushing his as he held her tight, rolled, thrust himself on top until the mind could no longer grasp the need, and only intuition, instinct could guide them to the final, the ultimate fulfilment.

When the shudders had passed, when breathing had returned to a bearable level, they sighed in unison, groaned, unclenched muscles and relaxed warmly against each other.

Lian's heart felt bruised, aching, as though it had worked too hard, had hurled itself courageously against the chest wall, given all that had been asked of it. Her lungs, in contrast, felt too small, totally inadequate for the task given them; and her thighs quivered as muscles were allowed to relax, return to the earlier inertia.

'Dear God,' Jared breathed against her neck.

'Yes,' she agreed with total inadequacy.

They lay, silent, for a long time, just savouring what had happened, the totally unexpected passion that had raced between them, raged to engulf them. Ardent, intense, uncontrollable. Their earlier kisses, teasing, at his home, had prepared neither of them for such a conflagration.

Moving slowly, as though she were drugged, Lian stared wonderingly into his eyes, then gave a shaky smile. 'And the earth moved,' she whispered.

Returning her smile with one that was equally shaky, he took a deep breath, and let it out slowly. 'How many years did that take off our lives?'

'Twenty?'

'More like fifty. My God, Lian, that was total fusion!'

'Yeah. Good, ain't it?'

With a snort of laughter he rolled on to his back and drew her warmly against his side. 'And no amount of money could buy that, could it?' he asked softly.

'No.' Had someone once before hurt him, taken him for a ride because of his money, she wondered? That was twice he had mentioned it.

'Two halves of a whole,' he went on, diverting her thoughts. 'Perfection. All the clichés, all the great truths, all the words that have been written about it since time began, and none of them come anywhere near explaining what has just happened.'

'No, because there *is* no way to describe it. There's only feeling. Love,' she added hesitantly, because there was still the fear that his meaning of love was not her own.

Turning his head, he searched her eyes. 'Yes?'

'Yes,' she confirmed. 'I've been in love with you for a long time. Oh, I told myself that it was only affection, desire, attraction, whatever, but it wasn't true. And yesterday, when I thought I'd lost you, I could no longer deny it even to myself. I loved you. Do love you,' she corrected quietly. 'And your son.'

Briefly closing his eyes, Jared took a deep breath, and held it. Slowly releasing it, he said, 'Thank you. As I love you, and Simon, who, as you know, is your adoring slave.'

Embarrassed, Lian gave a tiny grimace. 'I can't imagine why.'

'Because you don't use sham. Because you're honest, which he understood, and I sadly didn't. So many people over the years have tried to use him—to get close to me, to find out about my business, my lifestyle—that I'm afraid we've both become a trifle cynical. I *hate* people who do that, who are capable of using a child to further their own ends. Do you know that out of all the people I have ever met so few are genuine? I don't like being *used*, Lian, and I don't like people who are close to me being used either.'

'As someone did once use you?' she queried. 'Because of your money, your wealth?'

'Yes,' he admitted. 'A few years ago a woman I liked, thought liked me and Simon, and who turned out to be—grasping.' Turning to face her properly, he searched Lian's face for a minute. 'Perhaps that's what makes me ruthless sometimes.'

'Maybe, but I can be a bit ruthless myself,' she returned quietly. 'When it concerns me and mine.'

Amusement chased the seriousness from his eyes, and he gave a rueful little nod. 'Mm, I don't doubt it for a second. You are also, as I have reason to know, extremely generous. In spirit, in forgiveness—and now you're my golden girl with a wide smile and sparkling eyes, which brings me to something I wish to tell you. Simon and I had a discussion——' Breaking off, he frowned and held his head in a listening attitude. 'Was that the front door?'

Tilting her own head, she was about to deny having heard anything when there came the distinctive thud of the front door closing.

'It's only us,' her father called up.

'Only?' Jared queried comically. Disentangling himself, he rolled lithely to his feet, grabbed his robe and quickly shrugged into it just as Simon's distinctively elephant tread was heard thundering up the stairs.

'Dad?'

Making a lunge for the door before his son could burst in, Jared eased himself through the opening.

'Aren't you dressed yet?' she heard Simon exclaim, and, with a giggle, Lian quickly got to her own feet and hurried into the bathroom. Closing the door, she put her ear against the wood and shamelessly listened.

'I thought you'd gone for the day.'

'We had,' she heard her father reply in distinctly amused tones, 'but, in case you hadn't noticed, it's pouring with rain. We came back for our raincoats.'

'Oh.'

'And then we're going out to get ourselves some lunch.'

'Lunch?'

'Yes,' her father said drily, 'the stuff you eat at midday.'

'Midday?' Jared exclaimed, and Lian could picture his comical astonishment. Mind, she was a bit astonished herself. They surely hadn't spent the whole morning in bed?

When she heard the bedroom door open and close she eased the bathroom door open a fraction and peeked through the gap. 'All clear?' she asked a grinning Jared.

'Mm. It's lunchtime!' he exclaimed as though he really couldn't believe it.

'So I heard.'

Walking across to her and viewing the little he could see of her through the crack, he asked innocently, 'Is the water hot?'

'Hot?' she asked in confusion.

'Mm, I assumed you were running us a bath.'

Grinning widely, she threw back the door and invited him inside.

When Simon and her father returned they were sitting at the kitchen table eating a very belated lunch.

'Aren't you dressed *yet*?' Simon demanded.

'Nope,' Jared replied happily.

Glancing at her father, Lian grinned when he winked. 'Are we allowed to stay in now?' he asked blandly. 'I mean we don't have to go and view any more model villages? Museums? Boats?'

'We-ell,' Jared drawled.

For the rest of that day and evening both Jared and Lian seemed to wear a permanent smile. They glanced at each other often, laughed for no good reason, followed each other from room to room. When Lian went out to make a pot of tea, Jared followed her.

'I want to keep touching you,' he whispered, 'smiling at you—and, oh, lord, I want quite desperately to nuzzle your neck.'

With a little giggle, she moved her hair aside and presented her neck for nuzzling.

Standing behind her, his arms round her slender waist, he obliged.

Shivering with pleasure, she turned in the circle of his arms, slipped her hands behind his head and raised her face for a kiss.

'Oh, yuk!' Simon exclaimed from behind them. 'You're not kissing *again*!'

'Sure are,' Jared agreed blithely.

'It's disgusting!'

Turning to grin at his son, he said softly, 'Tell me that again in ten years.'

Leaning her head on Jared's shoulder, Lian smiled at his son. 'Time?' she asked him.

Glancing at his watch, which her father had bought him when his other one had been ruined by sea-water, he announced, 'Ten-oh-five.'

'Right, jarmies on, bed.'

Staring at her, he suddenly gave a slow smile. 'You sound like my mother,' he said softly.

Filled with mixed emotions—worry, fear, pleasure— Lian wondered if she'd blundered. 'Oh, Simon, I'm sorry, I didn't mean——'

'No!' he interrupted. 'I like it.' Looking slightly embarrassed, he hurried across and gave them both a hug. ''Night. Jarmies,' he giggled as he went out.

'Well, at least he wears them,' Jared murmured, tongue-in-cheek.

'Mm, want me to?' she asked suggestively.

'Yeah. Black satin?'

Grinning at each other like idiots, they giggled when her father walked in and gave them a look of disgust.

'Oh, my God, you're not still at it? I'm going to bed.'

''Night,' they murmured in unison, and then got back to the really enjoyable business of making love.

'Bed?' Jared asked hopefully.

'Oh, what a good idea.'

'Jared?' Lian murmured.

'Mm?' he mumbled sleepily.

'Does Simon remember his mother?'

'Not really, I don't think.'

'But he said...'

'That you sounded like her. I don't think he meant her personally, just someone who sounded the way a mother should sound.'

'Oh!' she exclaimed in pleased surprise.

With a little chuckle, he burrowed more warmly against her and promptly went to sleep. Bunching the pillow more comfortably beneath her neck, her foolish smile still in place, she thought over the extraordinary events of the day. She'd never felt like this before, never loved like this before, and she wanted to savour it, wanted to recall all that had been said, all that had been done, recall all the sensations. She felt smug, and warm, and safe—and a little bit afraid that it was all too good to be true. That to accept this happiness was tempting fate. Telling herself not to be a fool, not to be so suspicious, she snuggled against him and closed her eyes.

They made a supreme effort the following morning, and actually joined the other two for breakfast. Just as they were finishing the phone rang, and, with a smile, Lian went into the hall to answer it. When she returned she was laughing delightedly. 'You'll never guess who that was!' she exclaimed. 'Southern Television!'

'Southern Television?' her father asked in confusion. 'What on earth did they want?'

'Me!'

'You? Whatever for?'

Staring at them in turn, she shook her head in bemusement. 'I can't *believe* it.'

'Believe what?' Jared asked quietly.

'They want me to commentate on the round-the-world yacht race! Speak to all the skippers on the ship to shore. Meet with them when they dock at the end of each leg. Cover the whole damned race! I can't believe it,' she said again. She didn't notice the sudden stillness round the table, didn't notice their expressions.

'And the race takes a year,' her father said quietly.

'Yes,' she agreed, her smile still in place as she continued to think about the offer.

'And what about us?' Jared asked.

'What?' she murmured blankly.

'Us,' he repeated.

Focusing on him, she shook her head in puzzlement. 'I don't understand. What about us?'

With a bitter laugh, he retorted, 'I don't believe you. I really don't believe you!' Shoving his chair back with an angry gesture, he got to his feet. 'If you have to ask, Lian, then you've just given me your answer. Simon, you wanted to go into Exmouth, didn't you? Then let's go.' Without waiting for his son, he walked out.

CHAPTER SEVEN

WITH a look of bewilderment Simon hurried to catch up with his father, and Lian stared after them in confusion. Then slowly, so very slowly, her face hardened. Turning to look at her father, expecting his understanding, she saw that he was wearing the same expression of bitter disappointment that Jared had worn. Even her own father. Did none of them understand her? Obviously not. Hurt, bewildered, but most of all beginning to be blazingly angry, she too stormed out. Hadn't she known that it was all too good to be true? Hadn't she *known* that?

There was a hard, tight lump in her throat, a burning behind her eyes, but she was damned if she was going to cry. Damned if she was going to explain herself—to anybody. If they couldn't love her as she was... If they couldn't understand, believe in her, then they weren't worth bothering with. Taking a deep, steadying breath, she hardened her heart. How dared they condemn her? And it hurt! Dear lord, but how it hurt! After all their lovemaking, all they had said to each other, didn't Jared understand her at all?

Refusing to go back to the house for some money, she borrowed some from a local shopkeeper who knew her well, and then she just walked. Mile after mile, furious with them, hating them, and when she went back she would pack all her things and go, she decided. She didn't want people like that in her life! Her own father! Siding with Jared! Believing the worst of her! How could he? And how could Jared? Who'd professed to love her! Professed to believe that she loved him! Unaware, or uncaring that tears were pouring down her face, she continued to walk, and by late afternoon she was exhausted. She felt as though she'd circumnavigated Devon. Still reluctant to go back to the house, she sank down on the springy turf of the headland above the house. Staring out to sea, her vision blurred, she felt lost, abandoned, and so very misunderstood.

'Lian?' Jared said quietly from behind her.

Refusing to look at him, refusing to acknowledge him, she turned her head the other way.

When he sank down beside her and put his hand on her arm she flinched away. 'Don't touch me!' she said bitterly.

With a long sigh, he said quietly, patiently, 'Lian, we have to talk.'

'No, we don't,' she denied emptily. 'We have nothing to say.'

'Yes, we do,' he insisted in the same quiet voice.

'No.' Scrambling away, she got to her feet.

'Lian...'

Whirling to face him, her face set and hard, she blazed, 'You couldn't even ask, could you? Couldn't trust. Well, that isn't love! That isn't anything! Even my own father!'

Getting wearily to his feet, he sighed deeply. He looked exhausted. 'Lian, I'm sorry, but how could I have known?'

'By bloody asking!' she stormed. 'If you couldn't trust, then at least you could have bloody asked! But no! The great Jared Lowe just assumed! You automatically assumed that I would do that to you!'

'Yes, I did, and I'm sorry. I understand your anger——'

'Oh, do you? How nice! Jared understands my anger! Great! What a pity you didn't understand a few things a bit sooner!'

'Yes, it is,' he agreed with strained patience, 'but I didn't, and if you will just calm down and allow me to explain I will tell you why.'

'I don't want to know why! I don't want anything further to do with you! You hurt me, dammit!'

'I know——'

'And my father! My own bloody father!'

'Lian——'

'No,' she stormed furiously, 'just go away, I don't want to talk to you. And what a really nice opinion of me you must have,' she continued, ignoring her own injunction, 'believing that I would tell you one day that I loved you, and the next happily swan off round the world for a year! And the fact that you've finally realised that you were mistaken has come just a little too late!'

'I didn't,' he admitted honestly. 'The television company rang back to try and make you change your mind.'

Staring at him, Lian's hurt deepened, and she gave him a look of disgust. 'And if they hadn't you'd have gone on thinking the worst of me,' she retorted bitterly. 'Boy, you really had me pegged, didn't you? Well, I've a good mind to ring them back and tell them I *will* go!' Her throat blocking, her eyes filling with tears, she swung away. 'Go away,' she muttered.

If he had taken her in his arms then, allowed her to talk it all out, soothed her, agreed with her, everything could have been resolved; but he didn't. Like a fool, he thought it would be best to let her calm down, and so he did as he was told. He went away.

Left alone on the headland, she sank back down on the turf, wrapped her arms round her knees, and sobbed as though her heart would break. Wasn't anything in her life going to go right any more?

When she eventually returned to the house, after drinking endless cups of coffee in the village café, nibbling at an unwanted sandwich, it was gone eleven. Jared was in the lounge, obviously waiting, and with a withering look of dislike she walked out and upstairs.

'Lian?' he called.

Ignoring him, she hurried into her room. Miserable and aching, she curled up on the bed, and, hugging the pillow to her, she fell asleep—and woke two hours later to chaos.

Frowning, only half awake, she listened to the extraordinary sounds of someone hurrying back and forth. Out on the landing, up and down the stairs... Uncurling herself, she got stiffly to her feet. Opening her bedroom door, she peered out. Simon's door was open, the light on, and she could hear Jared's soft voice as he spoke with his son. She was still dithering on the landing when Jared came out.

'What on earth is going on?' she demanded in a heavy whisper.

'Simon's been sick,' he exclaimed worriedly.

Sick? Was that all? Walking along to Simon's room, she went in, and her heart melted. He was sitting hunched up on the armchair, a bowl in his lap, his brown eyes mournful. Ignoring Jared, who was hovering behind her, she walked across and put her hand on Simon's forehead.

'How are you feeling?' she asked him gently.

'I was sick in the bed,' he blurted out miserably.

Her eyes gentle, and smiling, she teased, 'Shocking. Think I should lock you in the attic and feed you bread and water?'

With a wan smile, he shook his head. 'I'm sorry. I didn't mean to do it.'

'I know that. Still feeling sick?'

'No. Yes. I don't know. Oh, Lian, I feel horrible.'

'Then we'd best set about making you feel better, hadn't we?' Turning to Jared, she said stiffly, 'Go and put the kettle on, then make up a hot-water bottle and some weak tea, not too much milk. He will also need clean pyjamas.' Turning back to Simon, she removed the empty bowl he was clutching and put it on the floor. Holding out her hand to him, she helped him to his feet. 'Come on, let's get you cleaned up.' Leading him out and along to her own bathroom, she sat him on the edge of the bath. Running warm water into the basin, she wet the flannel, then, whisking off his jacket, she gently sponged him down. He looked like a beaten puppy, and she wanted to hug him, tell him it was all right, only of course it wasn't.

When Jared brought his clean things in she left him to help Simon into them. Walking back to his bedroom, and keeping her mind blank, she stripped the bed and dumped the soiled linen out on the landing to be dealt with later. Collecting clean sheets and two spare blankets, she re-made his bed, and when he and his father returned she gave the boy a gentle smile and tucked him up. 'I'll put the bowl down beside you, just in case.' She was aware of Jared going out, but not by look or gesture did she ever acknowledge having even seen him. Perching on the edge of the bed, she smoothed Simon's damp hair back from his forehead. 'All right now?'

'Yes, thank you. Are you still angry?' he whispered.

'No,' she denied without being sure whether she was or she wasn't. The last few minutes hadn't given her time to think about herself or her own concerns.

'And you aren't going away?'

'No.' Well, what the hell else could she say?

When Jared returned he was carrying the hot-water bottle and a cup of tea. Smiling at his son, he tucked the bottle in beside him and put the tea on the bedside cabinet. 'I'll be back in a few minutes. OK?'

'Yes.'

When he'd gone Lian too got up. She felt as lost and sad as Simon looked. 'Drink your tea slowly, hm? Just sip it, but if it makes you feel sick again just say and we'll try something else.' Bending, she dropped a light kiss on his forehead. 'Shout if you need me.'

Going out, intending to take the bedding down and wash it through, she found that Jared had already done so, and was waiting for her on the landing. When she went to walk past, he caught her arm.

'How long are you intending to go on punishing us?' he asked quietly. 'Because it isn't only me you're hurting, but your father and Simon as well.'

And herself. Her eyes wide and unhappy, she gazed at him, and when he reached out and drew her gently into his arms she went willingly.

'I'm not trying to minimise our behaviour,' he said softly against her hair. 'We were at fault, but misunderstandings are part of life, part of living, and all you had to do was tell us we were wrong. Been angry, yes, we deserved that, but I don't think any of us deserved to spend a day of misery and anguish—and worry. Not knowing where you were, if anything had happened to you. And I can't spend the rest of my life watching what I say; I have to be myself, we both do. There'll be other misunderstandings, of course there will. I'll probably shout at you, and you will no doubt shout back, but at the *time* of the misunderstanding, not hours later after brooding about it. It has to be instant, Lian, sorted at the time.'

'But you should have known,' she whispered miserably. 'So should Dad.'

'Perhaps. I can't speak for your father, only for myself.'

'But you thought I'd willingly, carelessly throw away what we'd shared; that's what hurt. That our lovemaking had meant so little to me that I would immediately throw you over when the sea beckoned.'

'Of course I did,' he insisted, giving her a little shake, 'because the sea was your first love, your first need, and there's still a part of me that wonders if I'm second-best. I love you, Lian, but loving makes you vulnerable. And I have such an overwhelming feeling of need that it frightens me.'

'It does?' she asked hesitantly. It was how she felt, but hadn't understood that he did too.

'Yes, of course. You once asked me if I ever wanted to marry again; well, I did, Lian. Once over the shock and pain of losing Penny, I did; it's what I've always wanted, for there to be someone there for me, someone to love, to hold, to share, only I despaired of ever finding her. And then you came along, someone else who loved sailing, and so I suppose I mentally made conditions. Was subconsciously always looking for reasons not to like you too much. And then, when I did finally admit that I was in love with you, I found it hard to believe that you could feel the same. And always, at the back of my mind, was this little voice saying, second-best. The sea was your life, you had told me that.'

'But that was before I fell in love with you. And anyway it wasn't second-best. They were two separate things.'

'Using logic, yes, but I don't seem to use much logic where you're concerned. And sometimes I feel about as confident as a cuckoo waking up in the wrong nest. I've never felt like this before, never had this over-whelming feeling of need, this fear of being deprived, and it screws my judgement.'

'But you loved your wife!' she exclaimed con-fusedly. 'Are used to being married, having a relationship.'

'Yes, but it was in a different way. She was sweet, gentle, and I suppose my love for her reflected that. I felt protective towards her—I didn't feel over-whelmed, as I do with you.'

'Do you?' she asked in a funny little voice.

'Yes,' he admitted gently.

Leaving that for the moment, she pointed out, 'But that can't apply to Dad. He knows me better than anyone.'

'Yes, and knew of your love, your commitment to the sea.' Easing her away, Jared framed her desolate face with his hands and looked down into her lovely eyes. 'For most of your life you had one goal, one ambition, and when it was taken away from you, although you tried bravely to cope, to come to terms with it, part of you was missing. Our love, our feeling for each other is a new thing, another beginning, another goal, if you like, and because it was new neither I nor your father could be sure that it would replace your other feelings. Not so soon, or so completely, anyway.'

'But that's what I keep trying to tell you,' she wailed. 'It doesn't replace them. They're entirely different things! If I had to choose, right this minute, you *know* what I would choose. Giving up sailing is as *nothing* compared to how I felt yesterday when I thought I was giving up you.'

'You won't be allowed to give up me,' he insisted, 'because I'll fight tooth and nail to prevent it, and if that's arrogant, then so be it, but I would use every weapon in my armoury to keep you—even if it means letting you go off to commentate on the race. When I stormed off earlier I didn't even get out of the village before turning back, before realising what a fool I was being. Simon was crying, bewildered, not understanding anything that was going on, I was furious, with myself as well as you, then frightened, and when I got back to the house, found you were gone, I spent the rest of the day looking for you. Where on earth did you go?'

'I don't know,' she confessed. 'I just walked—anywhere, everywhere.'

With a little nod, as though he understood, he continued, 'And while I was looking, worrying about you, I began to work out ways and means of remaining together. If it meant so much to you, I decided, then I would go too, and Simon. Hire private tutors. Reorganise my business.'

'Oh, Jared!' Lian exclaimed helplessly. 'If terms had to be attached, it wouldn't be loving.'

'Of course it wouldn't, but you wouldn't *make* terms, would you? I knew that, and when I'd calmed down and began to consider things rationally I knew you wouldn't just rush off and leave us. No, I assumed you were desperate to go, and that, for a moment, you had forgotten me. I thought that when you'd realised what you'd said you would be contrite, unhappy, and so I decided to make this really great gesture so that you could go and do what you really wanted.'

With a wry smile he added, 'I would, I think, do almost anything to make you happy, do anything for you; so would Simon, because we both love you, and I don't think either of us can quite believe our luck—that after searching for such a long time we finally found you. Can't quite believe that you would love us back in the same way.'

'You make me sound special,' she exclaimed worriedly, 'and I'm not.'

'Yes, you are. To us you are very special. You're our kind of person. You belong. Make our lives complete. So, are we forgiven?'

With a jerky little nod, she rested her head against him.

'And next time when I get things wrong tell me. You can point your finger, shout, whatever, say, "Now look here, Jared, you're way out of order," and that's OK, because then it can be discussed, thrashed out; but don't walk away, Lian, don't ever leave the pot boiling.'

You did, she wanted to point out, but perhaps that wouldn't be altogether wise. He'd apologised, and she knew, finally understood, that she would lose more by arguing further than she would ultimately gain. A loving relationship was built on give and take. If Jared loved her enough to let her go, then she loved him enough to forgive, or ignore, his arrogance. Lifting a finger to his mouth, she gently traced his bottom lip. 'I love you,' she whispered.

'And I love you. So very much. Now, let's go and make our peace with Simon.'

Feeling guilty for the hurt she'd caused his son, Lian asked, 'Is that why he was sick, do you think?'

'Maybe. Although,' he added with a faint twinkle in his dark eyes, 'he did say that the hamburger he had for lunch tasted a bit funny. Now, come on, before he thinks we've both deserted him. Your father, I'm afraid, will have to wait until the morning. When I looked in on him a few minutes ago he was sound asleep. Or pretending to be. Giving her a swift, hard kiss, Jared tugged her back into his son's room.

'How are you feeling?' she asked Simon gently.

'Much better. I don't feel sick any more.' Glancing at his father, then back to her, he asked hesitantly, 'Is it all right now? Has Dad told you?'

'Told me what?' From the corner of her eyes she saw Jared give a little shake of his head and mouth something. Simon grinned and snuggled under the covers.

'I think I'll go to sleep now. 'Night.'

With an answering grin, Jared bent to kiss him, then, waiting while Lian did so, he held out his hand to her. 'Come on, we have things to discuss. Simon and I have had this really brilliant idea.'

Somewhat bemused, she took his hand, smiled at Simon, and allowed herself to be led back to her room.

Closing the door, Jared drew her into his arms.

'Is this the good idea?' she asked huskily.

'One of them.' Lowering his head, he parted her mouth with such gentleness, such hunger, she felt tears blur her eyes.

Hugging him fiercely, she deepened the kiss, held him impossibly tight, and when they'd finished kissing, to the entire satisfaction of them both, Jared urged her towards the bed, and, stacking the pillows against the headboard, he pulled her down beside him. 'Now, before we got ourselves into a muddle, before, in fact, Simon and your father interrupted us yesterday, I was about to tell you something.'

'Go on,' Lian encouraged as she nestled comfortably against him, her eyes on his dear face.

'I had just finished telling you how much better you were looking, how much the sea air obviously agreed with you... And if you don't stop looking at me like that I won't be able to tell you anything at all.'

'Sorry,' she apologised without moving so much as a nerve-end.

With a little chuckle, he continued determinedly, 'Simon and I decided that we also liked being by the sea. And your father, clever man that he is, and who knows you very well, despite the fact that you recently decided he didn't, has been—casually, you understand—introducing my son to some of the local lads. Lads, moreover, who just happen to be his own age, and would, if they all attended the same school, be in the same class.'

'And so?' she prompted softly as she allowed her lips to drift, oh, so delicately, against his cheek.

'And so we've decided that we would like to live here.'

Drawing back a fraction, Lian asked in surprise, 'In this house?'

'No, in Devon, but near enough for easy visiting. We also,' he persevered, 'decided, owing to the fact that you are a very strong-minded woman, that it might be best to present you with a *fait accompli*.'

'Meaning?'

'Meaning we have found a house. A very perfect house. It's not far from here, tucked rather nicely into the hillside, with river frontage, which we decided was a must, with mooring, naturally. It has five bedrooms, two reception, kitchen, two bathrooms, laundry-room, a small dwelling in the grounds that would be ideal for a married couple who might just like to garden and housekeep. It is also, miracle of miracles, on a bus route, and the local bus just happens to go past the school where Simon might just like to go and renew his acquaintance with all his new-found friends. All, in fact, that remains is for you to view it, give your approval, and say yes—to both questions,' he tacked on softly.

Staring at him, her eyes almost blank, Lian asked stupidly, 'When did you go to see it?'

With a wry smile he admitted, 'The day we were late home.'

'You said you forgot the time!'

'We did.'

'But not because you were out sailing?'

'No.'

'You lied to me,' she accused.

'I surely did,' he agreed unrepentantly.

'Let me shout at you.'

'Mm, mm.'

'And you work in London. So how on earth are——?'

'I don't always work in London, but when I do, when I need to go up, there's a perfectly adequate train service.'

'Or helicopter,' she said faintly.

'True. And if I eventually decide to go back to engineering, then I'll also work out how to get wherever I have to be. No problem is insurmountable—I hope,' he added. Searching her eyes, he asked, 'Could you be happy somewhere like that?'

'Yes,' she agreed huskily.

'And do you think you will be able to find something to occupy you?'

A slow smile starting in her eyes, Lian nodded. 'Oh, yes, provided you're there too, of course.'

'Good,' Jared approved softly.

Still staring at him, she swallowed drily as her smile slowly faded. 'You said two questions.'

'Yes.'

'One being the question of the house? And the other?'

'The question of your becoming Mrs Lowe.'

'Mrs . . . You want to marry me?'

'Well, of course I do, you silly girl. What on earth did you think I wanted?'

'I don't know, I hadn't got that far in my thinking. It seemed just enough to know that you actually loved me.'

'Then think about it now,' he encouraged.

Which she did. Her eyes fixed on his face, she suddenly exclaimed faintly, 'Oh, my God—I'll be Lian Lowe! Oh, I'm not having that.'

'Lian L—— So you will.' His mouth twitching, he queried softly, 'Will be?'

'What?'

'You said, will be, not would be. Will. Does that mean yes?'

'Well, it did until I realised what my name would be. Oh, Jared, I downright refuse to be Lian Lowe.'

'Lying Low...' With a shout of laughter, he dragged her into his arms. 'Oh, I love it! Jared and Lying Low.' His large frame shaking, he buried his face in her thick hair.

'It's not that funny,' she reproved.

'It is, it is,' he chuckled. 'Oh, Lian, I love you. We have to get married, even if only for the joy to be had from seeing the expression on people's faces when I introduce you.'

'Well, that's a really good reason to get married, isn't it?' Her own lips twitching, she wriggled down the bed. Urging him to follow suit, when they were lying side by side, hugged in each other's arms, she eventually, and very successfully, diverted his thoughts into other channels. Much more satisfying channels— and it was no longer laughter that shook his large frame ...

Next Month's Romances

Each month you can choose from a world of variety in romance with Mills & Boon. Below are the new titles to look out for next month, why not ask either Mills & Boon Reader Service or your Newsagent to reserve you a copy of the titles you want to buy — just tick the titles you would like to order and either post to Reader Service or take it to any Newsagent and ask them to order your books.

Please save me the following titles:	Please tick	√
THE WIDOW'S MITE	Emma Goldrick	
A MATTER OF TRUST	Penny Jordan	
A HAPPY MEETING	Betty Neels	
DESTINED TO MEET	Jessica Steele	
THE SEDUCTION STAKES	Lindsay Armstrong	
THE GREEN HEART	Jessica Marchant	
GUILTY PASSION	Jacqueline Baird	
HIDDEN IN THE PAST	Rosemary Gibson	
RUTHLESS LOVER	Sarah Holland	
AN IMPOSSIBLE KIND OF MAN	Kay Gregory	
THE WITCH'S WEDDING	Rosalie Ash	
LOVER'S CHARADE	Rachel Elliot	
SEED OF THE FIRE LILLY	Angela Devine	
ROAD TO PARADISE	Shirley Kemp	
FLIGHT OF SWALLOWS	Liza Goodman	
FATHER'S DAY	Debbie Macomber	

If you would like to order these books from Mills & Boon Reader Service please send £1.70 per title to: Mills & Boon Reader Service, P.O. Box 236, Croydon, Surrey, CR9 3RU and quote your Subscriber No:..(If applicable) and complete the name and address details below. Alternatively, these books are available from many local Newsagents including W.H.Smith, J.Menzies, Martins and other paperback stockists from 9th October 1992.

Name:...

Address:...

....Post Code:.......................

To Retailer: If you would like to stock M&B books please contact your regular book/magazine wholesaler for details.

You may be mailed with offers from other reputable companies as a result of this application. If you would rather not take advantage of these opportunities please tick box ☐

WIN A TRIP TO ITALY

Three lucky readers and their partners will spend a romantic weekend in Italy next May. You'll stay in a popular hotel in the centre of Rome, perfectly situated to visit the famous sites by day and enjoy the food and wine of Italy by night. During the weekend we are holding our first International Reader Party, an exciting celebratory event where you can mingle with Mills & Boon fans from all over Europe and meet some of our top authors.

HOW TO ENTER

We'd like to know just how wonderfully romantic your partner is, and how much Mills & Boon means to you.

Firstly, answer the questions below and then fill in our tie-breaker sentence:

1. **Which is Rome's famous ancient ruin?**

   ❏ The Parthenon   ❏ The Colosseum   ❏ The Sphinx

2. **Who is the famous Italian opera singer?**

   ❏ Nana Mouskouri   ❏ Julio Iglesias   ❏ Luciano Pavarotti

3. **Which wine comes from Italy?**

   ❏ Frascati   ❏ Liebfraumilch   ❏ Bordeaux

Tie-Breaker: Well just how romantic is your man? Does he buy you chocolates, send you flowers, take you to romantic candlelit restaurants? Send us a recent snapshot of the two of you (passport size is fine), together with a caption which tells us in no more than 15 words what makes your romantic man so special you'd like to visit Rome with him as the weekend guests of Mills & Boon.

....

....

....

....

Mills & Boon

In order to find out more about how much Mills & Boon means to you, we'd like you to answer the following questions:

1. How long have you been reading Mills & Boon books?

❑ One year or less ❑ 2-5 years ❑ 6-10 years

❑ 10 years or more

2. Which series do you usually read?

❑ Mills & Boon Romances ❑ Medical Romances ❑ Best Seller

❑ Temptation ❑ Duet ❑ Masquerade

3. How often do you read them? ❑ 1 a month or less

❑ 2-4 a month ❑ 5-10 a month ❑ More than 10 a month

Please complete the details below and send your entry to: Mills & Boon Reader Service, FREEPOST, P.O. Box 236, Croydon, Surrey CR9 9EL, England.

Name: ....

Address: ....

.... Post Code: ....

Are you a Reader Service subscriber?

❑ No ❑ Yes my Subscriber No. is: ....

_____ *RULES & CONDITIONS OF ENTRY* _____

1. Only one entry per household.
2. Applicants must be 18 years old or over.
3. Employees of Mills & Boon Ltd., its retailers, wholesalers, agencies or families thereof are not eligible to enter.
4. The competition prize is as stated. No cash alternative will be given.
5. Proof of posting will not be accepted as proof of receipt.
6. The closing date for entries is 31st December 1992.
7. The three entrants with correct answers who offer tie-breaker sentences considered to be the most appropriate and original will be

judged the winners.
8. Winners will be notified by post by 31st January 1993.
9. The weekend trip to Rome and the Reader Party will take place in May 1993.
10. It is a requirement of the competition that the winners attend the Reader Party and agree to feature in any publicity exercises.
11. If you would like your snapshot returned, please enclose a SAE and we'll return it after the closing date.
12. To obtain a list of the winning entries, send a SAE to the competition address after 28th February, 1993.

You may be mailed with offers from other reputable companies as a result of this application. Please tick the box if you would prefer not to receive such offers. ❑